THE TOKOLOSH
DIARIES

RANDOM TALES OF A WHITE BOY GROWING UP IN APARTHEID SOUTH AFRICA.

Clyde Martin

TOMAS, DANIEL AND ROSALIE, THIS IS FOR YOU.

MARIA, THANK YOU FOR GIVNG ME THE COURAGE.

Lovingly edited by Sandy Lee Edwards

Cover art by Troy Wells

CONTENTS

Clyde Martin

ACKNOWLEDGMENTS

Thank you Greville and Lisa.

Thank you Cheron.

Mere words could never be enough.

THE BEGINNING IS THE END.

I
"LET THE WATER HOLD ME DOWN"

It was the sound that got my attention, two terrible different sounds, but it was the blood that eventually brought me back.

The second sound I had heard many years ago, it created instant fear. It was the sound of vertebrae snapping and breaking. This time it was my neck and the explosive sound seemed amplified a million times underwater. The first sound I had no idea where or what that sound was, or where it came from. It was a terrible sound, a dull wet thud.

The sound, however, was not the only thing that had my brain in a state of total confusion. A blinding light exploded in my head, an absolutely pure radiating bright white light that left me blind and confused for what seemed ages. Most probably it was only a second or two, I guess I'll never know, with certainty, how long I was out for.

Believe me, when you are in real danger of dying, time expands and slows down,

everything seems to move in ultra slow motion.
I know, that day, I most certainly should have
died.

The dull wet thud, I now know, was my
forehead cracking against an underwater rock at
my favourite surf spot in Jeffreys Bay in South
Africa. When I came around I was totally dazed
and confused.

I can`t remember falling off my surfboard. It
was a stunning hot summer´s day, the waves
were small and playful the water was emerald
green and we just had to go surfing. I remember
talking to George as the set of waves
approached. George caught the first wave and I
got the next one. I always wait for the second
wave, it´s just one of those things I do. I
laughed as I flew past him as he paddled back
up the point.

I knew I was in serious trouble when I saw the
blood. I had been in a kind of dream state
watching my hands floating and waving around
in front of me, I had no idea what was going on,
absolutely no idea where I was. What were
those hands doing slapping me in the face, what
I was doing underwater bashing my face up
against the rocks, the blood which was quickly
staining the foamy water was what brought me
to my senses.

The blood! The blood made me scared. Scared of what I had no idea just yet but it made me scared, as only lots of blood can. I knew it was mine and something bad was happening.

I had to concentrate, what the hell was going on. Why was the water so clear? I could see the seaweed, a fish darted into my vision then disappeared into the foam and blood, everything was happening in slow motion.

Ever since the army days I have had this recurring nightmare, I have never talked to anyone about it. It's been my nightmare, it's always the same it never changes.

I am in a tunnel underground, crawling away from the danger, the tunnel just keeps getting smaller and smaller, tighter and tighter and then it collapses. It is total darkness, dirt suffocating me, trapped, fighting for breath. It never changes.

I wake up in a sweat gasping for breath, I haven't had my dream for years but things have been stressful lately, business is suffering with the global financial crisis, family life is going down the toilet. I had just come back from the police station to report my house had just been burgled and all my furniture is gone, even the coat hangers and pegs have been stolen for God´s sake. I needed to go surfing.

Real life had become a nightmare, but why had my nightmare transformed into this new version, it never changes. I needed to breathe, there was no tunnel, no dirt but I was suffocating all the same. A couple more seconds and I would wake up and breathe, it´s just my dream, it never changes.

The blood, the seaweed, the fish, those horrid sounds! This was not my dream this was real, I was drowning in waist deep water and I needed to focus and fast.

 Survival mode kicked in at last and it all came back in an instant, I had hurt myself surfing and it was bad. All I needed to do was stand up and walk a few paces onto dry land. Help would be there soon, George was there, he would help.

Most probably only about thirty seconds had passed but my concept of time had moved into another realm, those rubbery arms and freaky hands that kept bashing around like a crazy rag doll were mine. Why in hell´s name did they not work? Just push me off the bottom and stand up for goodness sake.

The next few seconds I have no way of

accurately putting into words. I was by now fully conscious and aware of what was going on and my brain was working at hyper speed, while everything else was in slow motion. I was in about two feet of water face down bleeding copiously. The only thing that actually worked was my brain. My arms and legs just did not respond to instructions and I needed to breathe NOW.

The wave saved me. It must have been a bigger set, as it pushed through with more force than any other. Up to that moment I had been just floating around face down trying to get a grip on what the hell was going on. That wave was a life changer, a small foamy a few feet from the beach was by far the most important wave I had ever come across.

Every surfer has caught waves they will remember forever, I have a few. My first wave caught at Ballito Bay way back in 1973, The day of the oil slick at Garvies beach when we were kids in the 80's. The wave I paddled over at the South African National Championship in 1987 wanting the next one which did not appear. The giant I caught at G Land in 1997, my last wave as a pro in 1993, the list goes on and on. As a surfer, waves have guided my life and in those quiet moments when I close my eyes I can surf them over and over. However, that one small insignificant broken wave of foam, I will never forget.

The wave saved me. It hit me side on and rolled me over, face up. Breathe, breathe, breathe, instinct took over, I sucked in oxygen, water, foam, blood, absolutely everything I could. To this day I wonder how I did it, are we endowed with super powers when the adrenaline kicks in? Try sucking a glass of foam down your throat and not cough, that day I sucked in litres of foam and water without so much as a splutter.

Newton's law of physics states every action has an equal and opposite reaction, that day was no different. The backwash of that set wave pulled me off the rock shelf into open water in the channel between the Point and Tubes and much to my horror back onto my stomach and face down. My brain was still in hyper drive and things seemed to be speeding up, which at the time worried me a bit, but my brain was at maximum revolutions. I had semi filled my lungs with air, I had a minute or two to work this out. George was there he would come. Yes, George was there, he would come. GEORGE "where the hell are you", my mind screamed.

It's not like in the movies, floating face down.

No predictably outstretched arms and legs floating nicely on top of the water like a starfish. My legs and arms where hanging straight down, I could see them just waving around in the current, the same with my arms, what was wrong with me? Lift your arms and legs and swim, do something for goodness sake. Nothing happened, no reaction at all, just those seemingly boneless jelly arms and legs dancing around in the pink bloodstained water like some kind of freaky pantomime fantasy below me.

Think, think, think, have a plan work this through, brain redlining, heart rate just ticking over, I could hear it clear as a bell, dum-dum, dum-dum, dum-dum. I felt no pain, not a thing actually. Nothing and that was a terrifying reality.

If you have ever snorkeled you will know, underwater, there is a lot of noise and when your eyes are seeing everything in slow motion I promise your ears hear everything with the volume pumped up and the sounds were amazing.

That morning I did something I never do, it was a stunning summer's day, no wind, hot as hell, the sea was warm I could just tell it was. From the house you can tell, when the sea is that emerald green the warm Mozambique current has moved down the east coast and warmed the normally cold J Bay water to a very nice 20 Celsius. Why I chose to put on my wetsuit that morning is a mystery, normally I would have just run down the hill in my boardshorts, like I always do. There was no one surfing, it was small but looked fun. As I ran past George's door, I stopped and shouted for him to come for a surf.

I knew the wetsuit would keep me afloat even in this bizarre posture, torso floating, arms, legs and head all hanging down. I could see flashes of daylight as the gentle splash of the ocean lifted my head, ever so slightly, up and down. My mouth and nose was only centimetres from fresh air but I might as well have been at the bottom of the ocean for all the proximity of the air did for me. I must have been knocked senseless as my whole body had turned to jelly.

The feeling of helplessness is impossible to describe, fresh air and life was literally only centimetres away, all I had to do was lift my head and breathe. Come ON, concentrate for God's sake, concentrate. My life depended on moving my head five centimetres, nothing else mattered at that moment every single ounce of mental power went into that one single thought.

Just like that my head moved, it lifted a little,

not much but enough to raise my eyes and mouth half way out of the water and I managed to again suck in a small mouth full of water and air. I was by now floating out in clear water and by chance of luck I could see up the point, I could see George. He looked a long way away, he had his head down and was still paddling back up the point and away from me.

What made George stop paddling, sit up and look back, I am not sure. One day I will have to ask him, but he did. He sat there looking back at me floating like a sack for what seemed forever. It was getting harder and harder to hold my head up, I had to do something, I tried to call out.

The sound that emanated from my mouth was startling to say the least. This was just not my day, a series of grunts and groans, my tongue was like a slab of rubber in my mouth and along with pretty much everything else was just refusing to follow even the simplest of instructions.

Apart from confusing the hell out of me this really made me angry as I tried to call out for help. I made some really weird noises, but they got George's attention and he started to move towards me. He seemed such a long way away, too far away.

I had not read a book for years, I always was too busy, the twins, the surf shop, the business, the ASP, WPS it seemed never ending. I never even had time to surf anymore. Why I picked up that book a week earlier and read it cover to cover in five days, finishing just the night before, I will never know. I had been given it as a present and it had been just sitting on the bookshelf untouched for months. The reason I picked it up and read it still haunts me. Why I put on my wetsuit and why I read that book is a mystery I am sure I will take to my grave. Late at night when the lights are out and my mind is free, I still, to this day, continue to search for the answer.

The name of that book by Tim Winton is "Breath".

Breath, my whole life has been troubled by just that "breath". For as long as I can remember and especially when I was young, I have had trouble breathing. As a child I suffered with bad asthma, it has always been a daily struggle to breathe, an ever present, struggle for air. It never goes away.

I could see George coming towards me, slowly at first but as he got nearer and nearer he was paddling more and more frantically, he was still so far away. I was not going to make it. I had swallowed and breathed in too much water. I couldn't hold on any longer, my head slumped down and it felt like I started to sink. Reality and imagination from now on become a blur, I was dying, slowly drowning and I could not do a thing about it.

My life did not flash before my eyes, I could see the shafts of golden sunlight dancing in the water making amazing patterns on the sand below, my thoughts were crystal clear and I knew I would die. I was not afraid, not sad, not angry, I was actually at peace, almost happy.

 I thought weird things, I thought about my life insurance, my wife could sell the house on the hill, she would be okay. My boys would be okay and would be cared for. *My boys they needed me, they needed me, Rosalie needed me.* Concentrate, hang on, hang on, not like this, not today. I had unfinished business which I couldn't leave unfinished. I saw my wife`s face, my boy`s faces, they were worried and they looked sad, they gave me an inner strength, they gave me focus.

Breathe I needed to breathe, my whole life I had unknowingly been preparing for the next few seconds. The countless nights with asthma, the countless nights dealing with oxygen starved lungs. The memory of 1985 all those years ago when I had my lungs crushed, my spine smashed and I nearly suffocated to death on dry land, my tunnel nightmare, I always pulled it off, I could do this.

I felt a newfound energy, a new focus, everything was crystal clear. I put every single ounce of my mental power into one thought. Do not breathe, do not breathe, do not breathe underwater. Whatever you do, do not breathe underwater. I had just read the book.

The bright light started from the outer circle of my vision, slowly at first but increasingly brighter and brighter, becoming increasingly smaller and smaller. The smaller my circle of vision got, the brighter the light became, the brighter the light got the quicker it closed, until in a flash of white, everything switched OFF.

No, there was no tunnel of light, no cool guy in robes standing with a smile on his face to greet me, just a black nothing.

What happened next is just a big confusing mess, George was there, out of focus inches from my face speaking to me, but the volume was off. I could see his lips moving but nothing was registering. Then BANG the sound was back on, I had no idea what he was saying, I tried to talk, but again my tongue was still on strike, just garbled sounds. I could see fear on George's face, this snapped me back and words came out of my mouth, I can't be sure what he was asking or what I said. I know I was swearing at him for taking so long, that much I can remember.

Ever since that 3rd Feb 2009, I have sat and stared at the ocean from those rocks down at Tubes, I have run this through my mind a million times, tried to work it out. How long was I under the water? How did I survive? Why did I wear a wetsuit? What if George had arrived ten seconds later? Just questions, never any answers.

From out of nowhere a longboard appeared, George and someone else were rolling me onto it and they started moving me towards the beach as they worked their way through the surf zone, a set of waves broke. My surfboard, which was still attached to my left foot on its leash, was being dragged behind me like some kind of bizarre accessory to this whole drama and it came crashing into us with the foam of that wave. It crashed nose first into me, the pointed nose digging deep into my leg, it should have hurt like hell. I did not feel a thing.

I had spent twenty four years trying to forget

the last time I had been dragged from disaster on my surfboard, but right then it all came flooding back. Lt Le Roux was there for me in 1985, my surfboard had saved my life and spine then. Some things you can never forget no matter how hard you try. The memories flooded back, I could not believe it.

It was happening again.

They say fear is all in the mind. Bullshit I say. Fear is a real tangible touchable thing. People watching Discovery Channel who cover their eyes when they see a spider or a snake, no that is not fear. No, not that fear. Real fear based on real life events, the kind of fear you silently fight every day, the kind of fear that keeps you awake at night, the fear that drives your nightmares, the fear that changes your life. When that fear strikes there is not a thing you can do.

I was being dragged up the beach, we had made it in through the channel easily and my mind was clear and extremely focused. Self-preservation mode was now fully activated. I had done this before. It came automatically, as if in a trance. I heard myself rattling off instructions, go up to Glen and Cathy's house, call the paramedics, don't move me, someone call my mother, get my phone and wallet from the house up on the hill, nobody panic.

A small crowd had gathered by now, I was lying on the sand on a slight incline. I was safe, on dry land. I had to stay focused, keep talking, keep talking, keep spirits up, don't show any signs of fear, tell jokes, keep talking.

Until now the struggle had been to stay alive, there had been no time for fear, no time for anything else. The struggle had been to float, to breathe. I knew now I was safe, I knew I was doing the right things, it was by the book. I had been a lifesaver, I had been a safety officer with a St John's primary first aid certificate. Just follow procedure, do not move, not even an inch, stay warm, keep morale up and get into a hospital as soon as possible.

How bad could it be? This seemed a walk in the park, the sun was shining, I was staring into an impossibly blue African sky, I was surrounded by friends. My home was just a few hundred metres away. There were no terrible sounds of impacting screeching, grinding, crunching metal. There were no sounds of screaming pain. There was no sign of collective fear and panic. There was no copious amount of splattered blood. There was no death. Compared to 1985 this seemed a walk in the park.

How bad could it be?

George was standing talking to me, I was watching him, he had my hand in his. He was talking, I was not listening, I had to force myself to come back, to concentrate. George had my hand in his, what was he doing, concentrate, concentrate. George had my hand in his, he was asking me to squeeze his hand, OH OK, yes of course.

Why, what for?

That was when the uncontrollable fear struck hard.

George squeezed my hand, I could see him doing it, I could hear him doing it. Oh My God, I could not feel him doing it and no matter how hard I tried I could not squeeze back.

Terror struck in the form of ICE, an icy cold came over me. There was no pain, my brain went into overdrive again. George was now fiddling with my feet, again not a thing. Those freaky jelly arms and legs I had watched dancing in the current just a few moments earlier were mine. At the time of course I knew that, the harsh reality just did not register. I had more pressing needs then. Suddenly I was cold, not even the harsh African summer sun could warm me.

Not fifteen minutes had passed since I had glided past George laughing on what most surely was the last wave I would ever surf. This time I was done, it was over for sure, the unthinkable flashed into my mind, I felt a twinge of anger that I had made it. It had been so peaceful under water, I had been ready, life had treated me well, it had been good. I felt so cold all of a sudden, a lifetime of emotions in such a short space of time. I felt so cold and suddenly, so very tired.

I know I am a logical person, science over faith any day. Logic, science and faith all kicked in at that moment. I had done this before I had lived through being told I would be paralyzed before and it had worked out. Keep positive, keep the faith, never give up. The emotional rollercoaster I felt on the beach in front of the channel at the Point that day is absolutely impossible to put into words. There was no pain and that terrified me, last time the pain was all consuming, nothing has come close since, not even the day I crushed and pulled the end of my right index finger off came close. There was no pain, it was very, very cold and it was terrifying.

I was going into neurogenic shock. The danger was very real and it was far from over.

II
"AND YOU MAY ASK YOURSELF WHERE IS THAT LARGE AUTOMOBILE"

My love affair with morphine had been brief and intense and right then I longed to escape back to that warm sanctuary. The ambulance had arrived, time had blended into insignificance. I have no idea how long it took to arrive, thirty minutes, an hour, an eternity. My mind was a mess, I was in hell and it was freezing cold.

He had drugs of course he did, the paramedic ambulance driver, I was going to need some of them.

It had not started well for him, the paramedic ambulance driver. There is no path down to the beach from the top car park up at the whale lookout. He had tried to come down through the aloes and bushes, had tripped, fallen and rolled down onto the beach much too everyone`s amusement. No, not a good start and it was going to get worse, a lot worse.

The pain also started about then, I knew that pain, it was unstoppable. It started while I was being moved into the ambulance, at first a niggling throb, slowly growing, ever growing.

I knew then this was not going to be easy when I had to convince him to use the rescue backboard and neck brace collar before moving me. I definitely knew it was going to be a nightmare when he refused to use any kind of medication until we got to the nearest hospital in Humansdorp. Yes "Humansdorp" about twenty minutes away, the town were the humans lived.

The drive in the ambulance was bizarre to say the least. I was all strapped and bundled up in my silver space blanket, still in my wetsuit full of beach sand on one of those nice bright orange rescue boards, neck, arms, legs all tied down and immobile. All I could do was talk, which I suppose could be best described as a one-way flow of profanities directed at the ambulance driver for refusing to shoot me up with a bit of pethidine. Yes, I knew what I needed "morphine".

After only a few minutes we pulled over, which was impossible, no ways could we be there already. Maybe I should not have said all those things about his mother.

Of course, we had not yet arrived we had just stopped to pick his kids up from school. They climbed in the back with me and off we went, to take them home.

I never got to see those kids. I never got to see the ambulance driver. I never got to see the doctor in Humansdorp. I never got to see anyone that afternoon, all I got to see was the point I focused on directly above me. I regret that, I wish I knew who they were, I need to thank them one day.

 In hindsight stopping to pick those kids up was a master stroke, I was starting to panic. Fear of what was coming was starting to take over. Those kids sitting next to me brought things back into perspective. I assume they were young, the age of my boys, they were inquisitive and calm. We chatted about what had happened, they asked me "why do you have a big hole in your forehead?" Really!!! A big hole in my forehead, holy shit, no one had mentioned that before.

Everything was so calm and civilized, was this an African thing, do African kids take blood and gore as just another part of any normal day or was this just a normal day for these kids who had an ambulance driver for a dad?

My mind was working again, I had stopped obsessing on the pain and the fear, it was almost good, almost. Kids seem to bring things into perspective.

After we had dropped them off, it was only a few minutes more and I was being pushed through the doors of the hospital. I am not a religious person, anyone who knows me knows that, but when I heard the sound of those horrid hospital emergency entrance swing doors crash open as my stretcher banged into them, I closed my eyes and silently said a little prayer.

Is it just me, or do these crazy situations bring things into crystal clear focus. Is it looking death straight in the eyes that makes you sort the important and the bullshit out in a question of seconds. Maybe it's the drugs, like some magical serum that clears the debris from your brain.

You can do a lot of thinking when you can't move and can only see the same spot on the ceiling, maybe that's the reason. Back in '85 I sorted a lot of stuff out staring at the ceiling. I made some huge life changing decisions, not one have I ever regretted. Maybe it is the drugs. You can kind of look down on your life and see it for what it is, sort of like some crazy medicine man inside your head telling you the truth, telling you what needs to be done.

Yes, what needs to be done, I had a lot that needed to be done that day.

As I was being hurriedly pushed down the corridors through the hospital, I swear amongst all the millions of thoughts that were going through my brain at that moment, in the background I could hear the Talking Heads playing. I had not listened to them for years, this song was from the album "Stop Making Sense" we had listened to it that morning back in '85 at 121 Battalion. I suddenly felt an even colder shiver run right through my body.

I made a promise to myself then I would sort things out. Lately life had slipped out of control. My wife was threatening to throw me out. I had almost stopped doing the one thing that really made me happy, surfing. All I did was work all day, I never seemed to have time for my boys. I needed to make it through the day. I had my family depending on me. I had a lot to sort out.

I had a secret beautiful daughter in France that no one knew about. I really needed to deal with that. Meanwhile the Talking Heads turned up the volume in my brain.

"AND YOU MAY FIND YOURSELF
LIVING IN A SHOTGUN SHACK
AND YOU MAY FIND YOURSELF
IN ANOTHER PART OF THE WORLD
AND YOU MAY FIND YOURSELF
BEHIND THE WHEEL OF A LARGE AUTOMOBILE
AND YOU MAY FIND YOURSELF IN A BEAUTIFUL HOUSE
WITH A BEAUTIFUL WIFE
AND YOU MAY ASK YOURSELF, WELL
HOW DID I GET HERE?"

The blackmail was at first subtle, very subtle, I did not even realize it was even taking place, but once it had begun the screws got ever tighter and tighter. I had most probably been handpicked, a perfect target. Yes, a perfect target carefully selected and hunted down.

Thankfully, the doctor arrived. My mind was drifting off into negative thought. The pain continued to grow as the pressure of my wetsuit pushing down on my shoulders became a torture. It was weird pain, a new pain, a burning pain. Millions of burning needles being pushed into me, every single nerve ending was on fire.

Things speeded, up the lady doctor was good, she made things happen. Hundreds of questions, x rays, she kept me actively engaged in what was going on, she kept me positive but I could hear the concern in her voice. When she returned with the X rays her tone was serious, it was bad, worse than even I had thought.

I needed to go to Port Elizabeth, to a major hospital, nothing could be done for me here. She had called ahead, the neurosurgeon would be waiting, she pleaded for me not to go to the public hospital, but rather to go to the private hospital in Port Elizabeth. I had three different insurance policies, no problem, I was covered. It would take a little over an hour from Humansdorp to Port Elizabeth in the same ambulance with my same driver, who had, never for a moment had left my side.

I could not see her but I am sure she smiled as she pushed the needle into my right shoulder and said to the ambulance driver, "take him to St George's".

Miraculous and instant is the only way I can describe the effect of morphine. The moment you feel the sweet bite of the needle, the moment that liquid enters your body, tension and worry instantly disappear and the pain miraculously ebbs away. Amazing warmth grows from the entry point of the needle, it grows in ever increasing circles of pleasure, it is unstoppable and it is heaven.

I knew that feeling, I knew the craving for more would grow, I knew the magical effects would soon seem to last less and less, I knew I would soon want more. I had again crossed over into the realm of pleasure and pain. I was back in heaven, I was back in hell.

It was useless trying to fight it, it was useless worrying, the die had been cast, I had played my part. My fate was now in the doctors hands. I closed my eyes, the tension slowly slipped away and my mind wandered freely.

My life flashed through my brain, there were no constraints, no false moralities holding back my memories. They came in waves, as of course they would, random flashes, recollections of a short life.

It all came flooding back and at first it was amazing.

III
"AND YOU MAY FIND YOURSELF IN ANOTHER PART OF THE WORLD"

I am not sure how the handcuffs got into my possession I think they were bought by the boys for "Psycho Slut", the French groupie that had been stalking us for weeks.

For some reason they were in my Kombi, a Volkswagen T2, a gem of a vehicle. I know "Miss Piggy" had put them to use the night before in the car park in front of where we were staying at "Casa Ramos" up on the hill above the beach in Pantin. Everyone in the bar had marveled at how brightly luminous condoms can shine through a misted up back car window, but that is an entirely different story altogether.

The day had ended badly. I had just lost my heat at the Pantin Classic Surf Contest in Galicia, Spain. I needed a pretty low score and slipped and fell on my last wave, and was eliminated from the contest with an equal 17th place. I was not happy, I was used to a quarter finals finish or better, this was my last year on tour, I wanted another good result. I was pissed off.

For some reason there was a lot of green seaweed in the water that year, it was terrible. It was slippery and caused a lot of drag, I had decided to surf without a leash and had slipped and fallen on my first wave and lost too much time in that green mess. It was a bad error of judgment, a fatal error. I was not happy that afternoon.

Most of us travelled and lived in camper vans and Kombis, a small flotilla of vans following the European leg of the Association of Surfing Professionals (ASP) world surfing tour, we were a pretty tight knit bunch and were on a kind of permanent surfing adventure, from town to town, country to country, it was astounding really.

There were always girls around, they loved hanging out with us in the vans, they were not shy, far from shy. None of us spoke Spanish and none of them spoke English. That never seemed to matter, we all spoke a common language.

Grish and Spence, stopped at my van, they were going into town, it was going to be a big night. There was a rock band playing, everyone was going to Ferrol, it was Saturday night, summer and we had all lost that day. It was time to let off some steam. I thought about it for a few minutes said, right let`s go. I kicked the girls out of the Kombi and got ready. One of the girls

27

got back into the van and was making a bit of a fuss, I had no idea what she was going on about, but she refused to get out. Clearly, she wanted me to stay with her but that was not going to happen, I had a date out in town with the boys.

The handcuffs were on the stove. I handcuffed her to the bed, locked the Kombi, got in the car with Spence and Grish and we drove into Ferrol 20 km away.

Grish looked at me and smiled, he knew, he was the best player of all. Little did I know then, destiny was waiting in ambush in Ferrol that night.

It had all started with "Gorilla Biscuits" and Bullo a year ago in Tapia, or was it that first day in France in Lacanau when we stumbled onto the nude beach searching for good waves deep in the forest. No, of course not, actually it began the very first day I arrived in Europe back in April 1990.

I had never seen anything like it. South Africa was just so different, nudity was banned. Any kind of nakedness was not allowed, the Nationalist government had made it a criminal offence to print or publish any kind of nudity. We had been led to believe it was a sin and the

NGK church (NEDERDUITSE GEREFORMEERDE KERK) deemed any kind of moral misbehavior would most certainly end up with you burning in hell for all eternity. After my first night out in Newquay, in England, where I just happened to bump into a bunch of nurses on a hen's night out, I knew, if the church was right. I was damned.

It was Bullo in Tapia that started to keep a tally after "Gorilla Biscuits" and her friend had taken advantage of us while we were happily experimenting with the wonders of Cidra, the Asturian apple cider that was freely flowing in the bars of the small port town one night. We hardly ever paid for drinks, the bars wanted us there. Where the surfers were, that's where the action was and everything was mostly always free. They were crazy times.

I was in the first heat of the contest the next day, so I needed to get back to the Kombi, rested and ready for the final day. Cidra is like apple juice and it slowly sneaks up on you and when it hits, it leaves you in a mess. One minute I was fine the next I could hardly stand, I needed to get back to the Kombi. Bullo gave her the name "Gorilla Biscuits" and she came out of nowhere. I had not said a word to her all night but the moment I left the bar she came running after me. She was French, a yoga instructor and I was doomed.

Spence frowned at me and asked, "Did you just handcuff that girl to the bed" I laughed, they were´nt real metal but were just toy handcuffs and were broken. She could easily get out of them, unlock the van from inside and leave. Grish laughed, anything for another dot on the door.

Everyone knew what the dots on the doors stood for, we were the "Surfers from Hell, the Death Division" and we were on a wild rampage through Europe. I really cannot explain the feeling of freedom and adventure of those years. Before everything had been so structured, discipline was everything in South Africa, first at school, then the army. There were always consequences for any deviations and they generally involved punishment and pain.

Bullo started the tally. It eventually evolved to the dots on the door, but began with "Gorilla Biscuits" friend´s panties tied to the radio antennae of the Kombi, a trophy for everyone to see, proudly flown from town to town, country to country.

I never made it back to the Kombi that night in Tapia. I ended up in the backseat of a two door Peugeot 106 which was parked in the middle of the town square. "Biscuits" had helped me get there, I was in no state for anything and started vomiting like crazy, all over her, all over her car. Someone must have slipped something into my drink, I was dead on my feet.

I awoke the next morning with the blazing sun in my face, totally naked with a bunch of old women dressed in black shouting at me through the car windows. "Biscuits" had disappeared, it was late in the morning and I had no doubt missed my heat and an opportunity to earn a bit of badly needed cash.

That night I realized I was out of my depth, I was not prepared. Growing up in Apartheid South Africa had not prepared me for this. I had always considered myself a liberal thinker, we were a liberal thinking family at home in Durban.

I had vomited on "Biscuits" head and without so much as a blink she looked up and kissed me. Now that was a defining moment. That moment I realized I knew absolutely nothing and was about to enter into a whole new phase of education.

I will never forget that moment, it was brief, an instant in time but it is forever imprinted in my brain. She came across the park towards us, we had arrived in Ferrol. It was a glorious summer's evening, still bright daylight at 10 in the evening. We had arrived right in the middle of the town's summer festival and there were hundreds, no make that thousands of people in the streets.

She came directly towards me and we crossed paths, our eyes met just for an instant and I swear my heart skipped a beat. I had seen many beautiful women in Spain, there are swarms of beautiful women in Spain they are everywhere but she took my breath away. She was wearing an amazingly sexy Gaultier black leather waistcoat with silver pointed studs, tight fitting blue jeans, jet black long flowing hair, she was a goddess.

Our eyes met she walked past me and she was gone into the crowd. We crossed the park and went into the club. It was packed, the whole contest was already there, it was going crazy. Grish and Spence pushed in the crowd and that was the last time I saw them that night.

There are times when you can just feel it deep down inside, a kind of shiver a nervous thrill, you just know that something big is happening. It is not a conscious thing, like a deja vu kind of feeling you just know something is going to happen. The moment I stepped into the club that night, I got goose bumps and the hair on the back of my neck stood on end. Yes, it was going to be a huge night.

The Fish was there, Gill was there, they were ASP judges and they had a group of girls cornered at the bar, they knew I had just lost in the last heat of the day they called me over and offered me a drink. We were like a big travelling circus, they knew what I normally drank, Fish handed me a vodka and orange, looked me straight in the eyes and said, you take the short one with the blue eyes and I´ll take her friend with the big tits.

I swear in Spain there must be more bars than people, it has to be seen to be believed. You have a drink or two in one bar then move onto the next as you go along you collect more people into your group and lose others. The night never ends as it begins and never ends as expected. It's a real life living experiment of the "Chaos Theory" and it is glorious.

Fish, Gill, "Blue Eyes", "Big Tits" and myself were cruising, we had gathered quite a number of people in our pack as we went from bar to bar. Unlike Formula One, after every pit stop, you do not go faster. Your chances of spinning out just become greater and greater.

I was learning fast, this was not a sprint like
South Africa where everything closed just after
midnight or like the UK where the bars closed
at 11pm. This was a marathon, the discos only
opened after 1am and the parties lasted till long
after the sun had risen the next day. After the
shock of being abused by naughty "Gorilla
Biscuits" in Tapia, I had learned my lesson.
Pacing yourself was everything.

One of Spain´s biggest and best all-time bands
was playing in Ferrol that night and the town
was packed, the streets were full, the bars were
full. Once again, I felt that feeling. South Africa
had not prepared me for this, I had never seen
so many happy young people, freely walking
the streets, no restraints, no restrictions of any
kind. In South Africa we had just come out of a
"state of emergency" where martial law had
been declared and no one freely roamed the
streets at night. This was new for me.

That´s when I saw her again, almost in the same
place, this time we crossed paths going in
opposite directions. She gave me a sultry
defiant stare and the smallest of smiles as she
brushed past into the crowd. She was going to
the bar we had just left. "Blue Eyes" gave me a
dirty glance as I turned around and watched her
walk away into the growing crowd. At the last
possible moment just as she disappeared into

the mass of people going to the rock concert, she turned ever so slightly and looked back and smiled.

Bingo, it was game ON.

I have no idea how long the bar roulette went on for, it seemed as if the whole of Ferrol was out that night, we kept on bumping into people from the contest then losing them again only to meet up later somewhere else. The boys from Pukas in their Renault Espace, were on a mission, with Pablo and Ignacio leading their charge. They were the real masters at this game, I was just a mere apprentice, I could not keep up and always seemed to be a few paces behind them. Throughout the night they seemed to drift in and out of vision as we kept crossing paths, their car always full of laughing girls and raging surfers. If an award for the naughtiest guy on tour was awarded, Pablo would have been the winner hands down, if ever there was a problem Pablo was guaranteed to be involved.

The year before in Pantin we had drama in the water, it was a solid powerful ground swell, big lumps of ocean, perfect for me. I had, Pablo, Gorka and Jorge in the quarter finals. It should have been an easy heat, semis next, almost a sure thing.

We were sitting up against the cliffs and as soon
as the heat started I dashed into the middle of
the bay with Pablo sticking to me like glue, a
perfect big wave stood up right in front of me
and I was perfectly placed to get it, in the first
minute of the heat, a perfect start. I looked at
Pablo he was too deep, impossible for him to
go, he was famous for playing dirty, He was
paddling over the wave and shouted for me to
go, I turned paddled two hard strokes and was
up and gone. As soon as I committed he had
turned and thrown himself into the same wave,
somehow, he made the drop, bottom turned and
was right behind me. A classic interference, the
judges had no choice, my contest had come to
an end.

I was not angry, I was fuming, I wanted to
smash his head in, instead we were getting
caught by set after set and getting smashed
ourselves right up against the cliffs and rocks of
Pantin. Earlier in the day the contest had been
called off while one of the Owen twins rescued
another competitor who was drowning in the
middle of the heat, so this was not a game this
was heavy water pushing us up against the
rocks. My anger dissipated fast as survival came
first.

Eventually there was a break in the sets and we
made it safely back into the lineup. I was

swearing and cursing at Pablo, the other two competitors gave us both a nervous glance and moved as far away from us as possible, I said to them not to worry they would advance into the semis as Pablo was not going anywhere. I grabbed his leash, wrapped it round my arm and paddled him out to sea. He was not going to get another wave, not if I could help it.

We sat in open ocean for the next 25 minutes with Pablo frantically trying to get away but I held him like my life depended on it, the whole beach and every other competitor was watching, let this be a lesson. With a minute to go a perfect big wave stood up right in front of me, I let Pablo's leash go, paddled hard for it and went. It was a perfect wave I got a big score and just missed advancing to the semis by a fraction of a point. Pablo came last, the only wave he caught that heat was the wave of the interference. We had a little scuffle on the sand before we were broken apart and we went our separate ways.

So that night when I saw Pablo being chased out of the disco we were about to enter and down the road by a group of apparently very angry guys and a few policemen, I smiled put my arm around "Blue Eyes" and walked in.

Things went downhill pretty fast from there. It was packed, more and more people poured into the club, our group was growing by the minute. I have no idea how or why the owner of the club came over and ordered us all another round of drinks, he started talking to the Fish who by now was hardly able to stand and was drooling all over "Big Tits".

One minute we were all in the mosh pit, going berserk and the next we were on the stage, the owner was mumbling something to me and was handing me notes of cash. I had no idea what the hell was going on, Gill said to me dance, just dance, dance, dance.

Gill, who at the best of times was a bit creepy, was the one who started it. The stage had a kind of walkway, so like a bunch of dancing monkeys, we started dancing. The crowd was loving it and then all of a sudden went wild. I turned around to see Gill had started to rip his clothes off, I felt I had no choice but to do likewise.

I suppose there is a first time for pretty much everything in life and this was the first time I had literally hundreds of crazy screaming girls at my feet and they were shoving more notes of cash at us. The rest of our group were literally rolling around on the floor laughing, it was pretty hilarious. We were down to our underpants and people were stuffing money into them, it was the most bizarre situation ever.

I looked over at the Fish and "Big Tits" and there she was, talking to "Blue Eyes" staring right at me. She was the only person in the club who was not laughing.

Shit! she was friends with "Blue Eyes" and "Big Tits", I jumped down off the stage, managed to rescue most of my clothes, shoved the notes I had stashed in my underwear into my pocket, quickly got dressed and walked over to the Fish as if nothing had happened. Everyone was laughing hysterically as Gill tried to get naked and the bouncers pulled him off the stage and out the back.

I looked at her, walked up and said let's go, she said okay and we left.

We walked the streets talking all the while. The Pukas Renaut Espace was still cruising around like some kind of ghostly phantom. We sat in the park, and before we knew it the sun was rising, everyone had disappeared and I was stranded in Ferrol. She walked me to the taxi rank, pushed me in a taxi and told the driver to take me back to Pantin. I wanted to see her again.

The taxi driver was jabbering away the whole trip but I had half passed out in the back seat, I grabbed some of the crumpled notes I still had in my underwear, paid him and opened the door to my Kombi.

The moment I stepped in the sliding car door, she hit me and started yelling like a mad thing. Holy cow, what was going on?

I had forgotten all about the girl handcuffed to the bed, "what the hell" was she still there.

She was still handcuffed to the bed and had wet her pants.

The ambulance had stopped and the driver was talking to me. I had been forced out of that happy place, it all seemed so real as if it was all actually happening, but I was strapped to the stretcher again in the back of the ambulance.

The pain slowly coming back, little by little the burning nerves were being woken up, the fires had reignited in my shoulders and arms, was this a good thing? I felt nothing in my legs.

He was telling me he had to stop on the highway and I had to change to an ambulance from Port Elizabeth as this was as far as he was allowed to drive. It did not take long for the new ambulance from St George's hospital to arrive and on the off ramp to Van Stadens Pass half way to Port Elizabeth on the N2 highway, I was transferred to the new ambulance.

Of course, I tried my hardest to get the new driver to give me another little jab of pethidine. I so wanted to forget what was really going on and go back to where I had just come from. I was having such a good time, it felt so real. I shut my eyes, gritted my teeth and knew deep down inside I would have to get through the next three hours. It was always the same, the first hour is heaven, the second hour is bearable, the third hour the pain becomes all consuming, the last hour is hell. I knew they would be long hours, every second taking forever.

Thank goodness at that moment I did not know just how long they actually would become, because when the pain strikes back, so do the bad memories.

IV
"LETTING THE DAYS GO BY, WATER FLOWING UNDERGROUND"

When you are having a bad day they normally only just get worse, today was going to be no different.

I had been lying in my wetsuit for about five hours by the time we eventually got to the hospital in Port Elizabeth. I was freezing cold and the pain was getting out of control again. The silver foil space blanket was not keeping me warm. It seems impossible but the feeling of it touching my shoulders was causing me a lot of pain.

The ambulance driver wheeled me into the reception of St George's hospital and the second chapter of my bad day begun.

The nurse asked me for my health insurance policy number, which of course lying tied to a stretcher, head bashed open, neck broken, paralyzed arms and legs in your wetsuit, no identification, wallet, telephone, the last thing you would ever remember is your insurance policy number.

However, until you supply said information or pay in cash, you can moan all you like and you will remain outside tied to your stretcher.

Full of blood, sea sand, in a wetsuit and absolutely no way in the world would I be let into a ward to be seen by the doctor who was waiting to see me.

"Viva" the private health system.

My mother arrived and things started to move forward at last, she had been told what had happened and had gone and got my phone and wallet at the house up on the hill.

While she was harassing the nurse at reception, another nurse was asking me to fill out a set of forms, I am not quite sure if she was a retard or just did not care or notice I was tied to a stretcher and was in no able state to be filling out any forms.

She insisted however and eventually obviously had to write down all the information she wanted herself. As soon as she left the nurse who had been talking to my mother came over and asked me to fill out all the same set of forms again. That was enough! I lost the plot and started a morphine driven verbal tirade at the surprised hospital staff. I was drugged up to the eyebrows and in a hell of a lot of pain and she was asking me to fill out a set of forms, I had just finished filling out.

I heard Glenn giggling somewhere as my mother tried to calm me down.

The nurse had maxed out my three credit cards and was explaining, I had ten days of hospital care paid for but would need to negotiate a private deal on any of the treatments received by any doctors or surgeons and was now asking me to sign the credit card slips.

JESUS, this was like a Monty Python skit.

Just when I thought things could not get any worse another nurse came up to me and asked if I could fill out a set of forms before I could be admitted to a ward.

I could hear Glenn now laughing hysterically somewhere as I closed my eyes, took a deep breath and seriously wondered if it would not have been better if George had not just left me floating face down back at Tubes.

It seemed like a lifetime ago.

I was tied to the bed and placed in traction. The ambulance driver who, in his defense, had been amazing and had never left me for a minute all this time, asked to be paid in cash. He had somehow produced an invoice for R2000 and was insisting in being paid in cash before he could leave.

They finally cut my wetsuit off, damn it was brand new, tied a10kg weight to my feet and with a strange harness type thing under my chin and around my head tied another 10kg weight to my head. Just like the good old medieval days, stretched out on the rack and tortured to death.

Strangely it felt instantly better, thank goodness, my mother was there, she went and drew two grand out of the ATM. Funny that is the maximum withdrawal amount per day and paid the ambulance driver.

Finally, I felt I could at last relax. Did I mention, I truly dislike hospitals, way too many dark moments have I spent there, but at that moment, it felt safe.

I had been in a state of maximum tension for about five hours which even the morphine had not been able to suppress. When I was finally in bed and waiting for the orthopedic and neurosurgeon to arrive and the blankets had been pulled up, I at last let the tension slide away.

Within seconds I felt the nausea, the human body has an astounding ability for self-preservation, I knew what was coming next and asked the young nurse who was still hovering around the bed if he could perform a log roll as I urgently needed to roll onto my side. I had vomited face up after surgery in `85 and had almost drowned in bed, not today, I needed to get onto my side and quickly.

The moment I was on my side, I vomited a jet stream of seawater and mutton curry pie all over the helpless nurse who was still holding me. The force of it even surprised me. Until that point I had felt no need at all to vomit. It flew across the room and hit the far wall like it was coming out of a fire hydrant.

I had swallowed litres and litres of seawater trying to stay alive earlier, if I had vomited any time before being safe and in hospital the odds of me making it would have been so much smaller. The uncontrolled retching movement would have damaged the crushed vertebrae, damage that would more than likely have been so severe that they would not have been able to be saved.

Deep, deep down, somewhere in my subconscious, instinct to survive had kept me from vomiting until it was safe to do so.

The healing process and new beginning was about to commence.

The surgeons had arrived and were arguing on either side of the bed, I could not see them at all. The traction was working. Feeling had come back slowly but surely into my right leg, then left leg, right arm and lastly my left arm. It was still weird, not quite right and they were arguing as to what they should do.

The orthopedic surgeon was adamant, he said the bone damage was too big to fix, the loss of bone volume due to the vertebrae being squashed together could not be fixed. The neurosurgeon was of the other opinion and wanted to operate.

This scenario lasted for a week, every day I would go off for more X rays, MRI scans, more X rays and more scans. They would come back and have a good heated discussion in Afrikaans, I am sure they thought I could not understand a word they were saying. It´s kind of unnerving hearing specialist doctors talk about your future as if you were not even there, especially when you can feel them next to you but can´t see them. They would check the X rays and scans, then just go away, leaving me more and more confused and worried.

In the end the neurosurgeon came back and said he wanted to operate, he needed to rearrange the eight damaged vertebrae and place two titanium prostheses at the C3 and C4 level. At a later stage the same would need to be done for C6 and C7.

He kindly explained he could do three different procedures depending on the amount of money I wanted to spend, obviously the cheapest option being the least effective and the most expensive being the titanium prothesis option he suggested. He had written up the three different quotations for me to have a look at and think about. It took me about two seconds to work at which option I would be choosing.

I had, in the bed next to me, some poor soul who had completely lost the plot. I later learned he was a priest. I could not see him just listen to his uncontrolled ramblings. I had absolutely no idea what his problem was and surely he should have been in a mental patient's ward. He could not make any kind of sense, just random words in no orderly manner whatsoever came out of his mouth. I know I should not have laughed, but it was my only entertainment. The nurse would come and ask him if he was okay, if he wanted some tea, the answers were always the same, just random words, with a lot of profanities thrown into the mix. Maybe he had that Asperger's thing?

"Hello Pastor, would you like a cup of afternoon tea? "

"Red, fuck, apple, shit, cock "

Would be his reply, it was just too much. One afternoon he had a few elderly ladies come and visit him, they were from his church and inevitably left in tears.

My brother, Darren, had arrived from Cape Town to spend a few days at my bedside and keep me company. I asked him what was going on with the guy in the bed next to me. I was not even sure if he was real. With all the pain medication, was he just another dream, had he had a brain op?

Darren had yet to witness one of his bizarre scenes. He looked at him and said no he has a broken leg, why?

Apparently, he went into theater fine but when he came out of the anesthetic, the wires in his brain just did not reconnect up properly again. I had already decided that money was not a priority, I just wanted to be able to walk out of the hospital as soon as possible, if the surgeon had asked me to hand over my house and everything I owned I would have agreed, no problem at all.

I just could not help but wonder if the guy next to me had chosen the cheaper option.

She never came.

That truth struck hard, it was a devastating realization.

The fourteen days in hospital, she never came, not once. The message sent was crystal clear, it was over. My goddess was, leaving she had, had enough. She had been the love of my life and that pain was infinitely more hurtful than a few broken bones, drugs can`t take that pain away.

Maybe just for a few moments, the drugs do take the pain away, but all too soon it comes flooding back.

V
"AND YOU MAY TELL YOURSELF THIS IS NOT MY BEAUTIFUL WIFE"

She came back the next day.

I was feeling terrible with the Spanish summer sun baking down on me in the back of the kombi and the acidic smell of urine from the girl who had been locked in the whole night was horrible. There were thousands of people all around the kombi parked at the contest, it was finals day at the contest in Pantin and the beach was packed.

I heard the knock on the kombi door, it was almost getting irritating, the girls always asking to come into the van, almost.

I slowly arose, it was mid-afternoon already when I slid the door open. There she was as stunning as the night before, jet black hair, tight jeans and a t-shirt, if possible even more beautiful than I remembered, with that Gaultier leather jacket.

It's always a worry the next morning seeing a girl again, alcohol has a horrible way of distorting one's perception. Not this time, my heart almost stopped seeing her standing there,

she said she would come but I only half
believed it, but there she was in all her glory.

I was in a state as the kombi stank of wet
wetsuits, piss and alcohol. I had to get her away
from there. It was the finals day so we went and
watched a few heats of the competition and
talked and talked. It was my lucky day, she
spoke pretty good English so we managed just
fine.

Herbie had written me a letter from Portugal in
1989. Yep a letter, written with a pen on a piece
of paper that arrived in an envelope with exotic
looking stamps in the post a few weeks after
being written. In no uncertain terms he told me
to get my arse over to Europe as soon as
possible. He wrote it sitting at Supertubos after
a perfect 6ft session with him and only a few
other guys competing on the newly found
European Professional Surfing Association (EPSA) pro
tour in Europe. We had become really good
friends while competing against each other at
the South African championships and on the
South African Pro tour.

That letter was a game changer, the words
jumped off the page and drove deep into my
brain. I decided right then, I would be there for
the 1990 season.

Three years later in 1993, I was veteran on the EPSA, was about to finish the year 5th on the European ratings and had a goddess sitting in my van.

In the 10 years since I first went in to the army in 1984 until that moment, I felt as if I had lived a lifetime, things had moved so fast.

Surfing was pretty big back in the 80`s in South Africa, it was a school sport. Surfing clubs were all over the place and interclub contests were huge. I started surfing for Quick Motion Surf Club at Snake Park beach in Durban, but moved to North Swell at Dairy beach after a year or two, literally there would be some kind of surfing contest on every weekend in Durban. At the time North Swell was the strongest surf club in South Africa and to make the North Swell A team was huge, especially if you were from the Bluff.

Herbie lived in East London "Slummies" and had talked about the Gonubie Classic as being an all-time contest, so when the North Swell surf club sent the A team to compete, I was stoked, the "Slummies" girls had an amazing reputation and Gonubie an even better reputation for being wild.

The club had organized everything and we checked into the Gonubie Hotel right on the point, the opening function was there and it was straight into party mode. Girls were everywhere and outnumbered the guys at least three to one. The plan was the same, find the best single girl possible, for some reason the sexiest girls kind of get left out, and go in for the kill. No hesitation. I guess some guys must feel intimidated by the nicest girls. I honestly cannot remember her name, but she was blonde and sexy. We went for a walk outside and were making out on the wooden walkway that went towards the river mouth, where the contest was going to be the next day. If I had known her father would be hunting me down in a few hours, I would have just walked away and gone to bed like everyone else who was competing the next day, but she was a very insistent young lady and I just loved that.

She looked at her watch and did a Cinderella on me. She said had to be home early as she had a school hockey game early the next day and her father had said she had to be home by eleven.

It´s when things take a serious deviation from the norm that they become the times you remember. This night was about to get surprising, hilarious and terrifying all at the same time. The weirder things become the more exciting and stimulating it is.

We had finally got to the blonde princess`s house, the lights were on and her dad was waiting, so we stopped on the street corner out of sight. I was about to just say goodbye and leave when she grabbed my arm and said her room was upstairs. I must just wait a while and she would turn on her bedside lamp as a signal and I must climb up onto the window ledge and she would let me in.

Afrikaans girls are gnarly, they have an edge, that unpolished feel to them and I was about to find out they will do what it takes. It did not take long and in hindsight not nearly long enough, before the light in her bedroom came on. It was an easy climb up onto the small awning roof under her bedroom window. Strangely almost exactly the same as climbing up to my brother´s bedroom back at home on the Bluff, I always had to get in through his bedroom window if I sneaked in and out of the house and had no key.

She was waiting for me at the window in her pyjamas, that's when I realized things were not going to be quite like I expected. There were burglar bars on her bedroom window and no way could I just climb into her room. I guess she saw the confused look on my face, she just smiled and stripped off her pyjamas and stood naked on the other side of the bars looking at me temptingly with a very naughty smile and an evil glint in her eye. She looked me straight in the eyes and started swaying her hips in the dulled light of her bedside lamp, I gave the bars a good shake but they were solid, no ways was I getting into that room.

My brain went into a spin, what was she doing, why did she want me up here?

Clearly, I could not get in, now what?

Cool as a cat she strutted right up to the bars and pressed herself up against them and said, "come here"

Holy cow !!!!! How did I find these girls?

She then slowly turned around pressed her arse up against the bars and calmly whispered, "do it through the bars".

I nearly fell off the roof.

I could not reach!!!! I am not the tallest guy in the world and the bars were just too high for me. So, with my jeans around my ankles I climbed up onto the bottom horizontal bar. That was the trick from there, it was just right.

White arse flashing like some kind of obscene strobe light, to anyone who walked by. Hanging off the burglar bars like some kind of kinky thief. A perfect start to my first ever night in Gonubie.

I wish I could say it ended happily ever after, but of course it did not.

We made way too much noise, burglar bars creaking and straining under my weight, flesh slapping, grunting and groaning, it was just way too much noise.
As I was about to get into the short strokes, that's when the shit hit the fan.

At the same instant as all the lights flashed on I heard him scream **"WAT DIE FOK GAAN HIER AAN?"** from the front door downstairs. Just one glance was enough to know it was time to get the hell out of there. He was a big man, standing in his white underpants, tea strainer white vest and a pump action shotgun in his hand.

He seemed very upset.

(Wat die Fok gaan hier aan?") - Afrikaans.
"what the fuck is going on here?"
I would amazingly hear that exact same phrase
again later that same year at the Beach Hotel
Cabanas in Jeffreys Bay, but that's another
story.

This was not funny at all. I made the fastest
eject off the roof you could ever imagine. I
jumped into the hedge with my pants still
around my ankles, fell into the next door yard
and made an escape.

Jockey underpants and shotgun, gave chase, but
I was way too fast, they had taught us well in
the army. I took the long route back to the hotel
but knew this was far from over. He would be
back and hunting me down again the next day. I
would be spending the rest of the weekend,
running down from the hotel to surf my heats
and hiding out in my room.

I never saw her or underpants and shotgun ever
again and that was a relief.

Unfortunately, Sunday was going to be another
strange day in Gonubie.

My brother, Troy, was there with the North
Swell junior team, we all had to share double

rooms, Troy was in another room down the passage way.

I had made it through all my heats and was in the first quarter final heat of the morning at 8am on Sunday morning. I was down early for a practice surf but eventually lost and was out of the contest with an equal 5th place finish. I watched a few more heats and slowly walked back to the hotel for the huge big buffet breakfast, which I had missed in the morning as I did not want to surf on a full stomach.

I got back to the hotel at about 9.55am and went into the dining room, but they had stopped serving breakfast already and were clearing up. I was starving and was looking forward to stuffing my face with a full English breakfast. When they told me I was too late I was furious. Breakfast was included and it was open till 10am. I complained to the manager but to no avail and was turned away from the dining room and my breakfast.

When I went up to my room I was not a happy camper, I felt doubly ripped off. First in my heat by the judges, I should have been in the semi-finals, and now by the hotel and breakfast. I am not quite sure what went through my head at that moment, but I was busting for a big morning shit, so I walked into a room on the same floor as mine, climbed onto the nice wooden bedroom cupboard and took a huge dump.

I honestly have spent many hours thinking about how we all changed doing our National Military service, when we finished we did some crazy stuff, bad stuff, funny stuff, just plain weird stuff. I guess it twisted us all just a little.

It just did not matter, no matter how hard we pushed the limits, it never even came close to the real experiences we had to endure a few years earlier. No matter what we did it just did not seem to matter. Not for a second am I implying we were angels before. We were naughty little shits, but it was an innocent mischief. That changed after the military.

Having a dump on the cupboard of the hotel, did not even raise a moral question at the time, not for a second. They wanted to screw me and not give me a breakfast I had paid for, well, take a big shit on your cupboard, see if I care.

The rest of the world did not quite see it that way and when the cleaning lady came in to make up the room, the proverbial shit really did hit the fan. I had climbed down off the cupboard, gone to my room had a shower, packed my bags and left for the airport, oblivious to the carnage I had left behind.

Mouse is a big man, I mean a really big man and he was angry, he wanted blood.

He was the president of North Swell surf club and had arranged everything for us, the buck stopped with him. The cleaning lady did not take long to find the big ugly turd on top of the cupboard. Piss had dribbled down the inside wall and formed a puddle on the floor, from there it was not hard to follow the trail upwards towards the terrible smell.

Just by chance it happened to be my brother Troy's room and his cupboard that became the focus of all the attention. I had already left but the rest of the team were driving back to Durban later in the day and were left to face the music which was playing very loud by about the time I was boarding my flight back to Durban.

When they got back to Durban all the juniors were interrogated by Mouse, no one admitted a thing. Of course, they could not, they were all innocent. Troy went down and took the fall. He was banned from North Swell Surf Club and North Swell Surf Club was in turn banned from the Gonubie Hotel for ever.

No one ever found out who laid that turd. I was back at my home beach Garvies, on the Bluff, away from all the drama going down back in town. The mysteries of destiny, If I had been caught my surfing career would almost certainly been cut abruptly short.

Another Bluff action going unpunished and there were a lot more to come.

VI
"AND YOU MIGHT FIND YOURSELF BEHIND THE WHEEL OF A LARGE AUTOMOBILE"

It stopped in that exact instant, the playboy messing around, it all came to an immediate end, it had to end soon anyway, surely? At the same time the next few months became a moral marshland of doubt and uncertainty.

My surfing career was over, it should never have even happened really. The surfing career, that is. It was time to move on and get back to a normal life. I was at the top of my game, as good as I would ever be as a surfer. I was ready to walk away from it all. My life was all set up for me back in Durban, my bachelor party had literally lasted for three full years.

In just two months, I was getting married to the most amazing woman you could ever imagine.

Moments, big ones, small ones, important ones, insignificant ones, they all add up and make life interesting.

 Life, just a combination of moments and they are all of equal importance, they make us what we are. They either prepare us for the tough times or they do not, and you never know when those moments are about to happen.

The moment I slid open the Kombi door that hot summer's day, and saw her standing there, a goddess with a nervous smile. Deep down in my stomach I just knew, I just knew this was an important moment.

I wasn't expecting it and I most certainly was not ready to deal with it.

It should have been easy really, just get in the car and drive off into the sunset. I mean it's not as if I had not done this before. If you liked her you got her number and promised to call her next year. Going back was not part of the plan, not even for a goddess. You never went back. This time there would be no next year, it was over for good. The best four years of my life.

In two months, I would be home. The tour would be over, a top five place finish on the European Pro rankings and I would be walking down the aisle. It was all planned and plotted out perfectly. I had lived out my dream it had been better than I could ever have expected. Real life awaited me. The life everyone expected of me, the life you have to have. So that's exactly what I did. I got her number, said

I would see her next year and drove off into the sunset.

Portugal was next. The long drive down to Portugal and the next event, I was having a good year I needed to focus on the job at hand but the moment I drove up the hill out of Pantin and thought of Portugal, I smiled. Fuck how much fun did we have in Portugal.

The first time I ever drove down to Portugal it was with Bullo. It´s over a thousand kilometres drive from Hossegor down to Ericiera and we had no clue where we were going. We were in convoy with the other South Africans, Herbie was in the "Big Blue" and Georgie and Katzy were in the "Green Mamba". All of our vehicles had names, of course they did, they were family.

I was starting to get the feel of this whole new European thing, the sense of freedom. I had survived Newquay, then France, well not France, but we will get to that some other time. We had made a few forays into Spain, surfed in San Sebastian, did the Mundaka run, had surfed it´s flawless perfect river mouth wave with no one out. Life pretty much could not have been any better.

It´s funny how you imagine places before you actually ever get to see them, sometimes they are way better than you think, sometimes it`s just a huge disappointment. France was better than even my vivid imagination could picture, the UK and Newquay were just horrible, but fuck me sideways, there were a lot of ladies around and that kind of made up for the rest for a short while.

Spain just left me breathless, we had done the Pamplona run as well as traveled up and down the coast. It´s pretty obvious by now I had this thing for brunettes and my hat, there were a lot of brunettes in Spain.

Anyway, I was excited to be going to Portugal, Herbie had written to me from Supertubos in Portugal, I wanted to go there, I just knew I would love that place.

It all started about a hundred kilometres outside of Burgos on those long straight roads heading west into the sun.

We had stopped for supplies, the first and last time I have ever been there. That was the glory of travelling in the van, it has everything a stove, fridge, table, bed, washbasin, pretty much everything you could wish for. While one of you was driving the other guy could make coffee, lunch, whatever, you did not have to stop.

It was in a small butcher shop in Burgos that I saw the single most beautiful women I have ever seen, she was just drop dead stunning. We had gone in to get some cold meats and some chicken and there she stood behind the counter in her blood stained white butcher`s overcoat and bloody yellow gloves. Jet black long hair tied up in a bun with her snowy white neck showing. That was all I needed to see, just a glimpse of her neck and I knew hands down she was the most beautiful woman I had ever seen.

Neither Bullo or I spoke a single word of Spanish, we pointed and mumbled in English what we wanted, she laughed and giggled at us making fools of ourselves, we paid and left. We still had a long drive ahead of us.

It all started to go horribly wrong when Bullo threw the first egg out of the window. If history has taught us one thing it is this, the surprise attack, the Blitzkrieg is extremely effective.

The first blow is always the most important but if you are going to throw it, if you attack, make damn sure you make it a telling blow, take your adversary down in those first moments of combat. If you do not take him down, trouble will inevitably follow.

Bullo had made the perfect first strike. The egg splattered all over the "Green Mamba" the looks of terror and surprise were worth their weight in gold. We won that first round and the next few after that. Bullo went on a mission, however, we soon ran out of food to throw. It became serious, deadly serious, when Bullo, decided it was time to roll the dice and had a shit in a plastic bag and lobbed that all over the side of Georgie's "Green Mamba". We were just cracking up, this absolutely was the funniest journey we had done in a while. We had the Guns and Roses blaring full blast, our cheap speakers threatening to blow a fuse, the miles were just flying by, this was going to be a trip to remember.

However, history also should have taught us if your enemy has superior weapons and you do not take him down and then leave him to regroup, it's just a question of time before he comes and seeks revenge. Invariably it is swift, devastating and unpleasant.

The "Green Mamba", was vastly superior to our slow older version of the Kombi and as we saw it speed off into the distance soiled and damaged, we realized that it had a roof turret and Katsy was standing tall and defiant as he stared us down as they accelerated away from us, bent on revenge.

I am not sure which is worse, knowing you are going to get punished and just sitting it out, waiting to take your beating, like when we were at school. You would get told you had been busted first thing in the morning but would only get whipped five minutes before you went home. You had to sit and suffer all day waiting to feel that biting pain of the bamboo cane, ripping into the soft flesh of your buttocks.

The alternative is of course thinking you had got away with your crime, then with no warning whatsoever, just when you are breathing freely, punishment is dealt out with swift brutality giving no time to prepare. This also happened at school at lot. The more psychotic teachers had a specially prepared cricket bat and it would strike without any warning whatsoever.

Suddenly bearing down on us at full speed coming directly towards us was George, Katsy and the "Green Mamba". Katsy had a suspiciously large object in his hand as he stood tall in the turret speeding towards us. It was kind of like a medieval joust with the two knights charging towards each other, except we had no lance, no shield, we were defenseless.

George put his foot down flat and accelerated to maximum speed at that precise moment, his bomb flew straight and true.

The explosion as it hit the windscreen was astounding, shit, flour, milk, piss, everything was in that packet as it exploded not on the windscreen but blew the windscreen into a million shards of broken flying bits of safety glass. It then exploded inside the van, an evil, smelly, precursor to the bunker buster.

How we survived? I honestly do not know, but we were fucked, proper fucked.

Three years later, this time alone, driving south, down to Portugal. I felt the same, fucked, proper fucked. The reality of the whole situation had suddenly hit home, the party was over. It stopped with the goddess.

I had four more contests to go, then I would go home and get married a no brainer really, life was good, better than it had ever been, better than I ever could have imagined. "Fail to plan, plan to fail" was what those tapes my dad had given me had driven into my brain, I just never expected it to be so much fun.

I have no idea how I did in that contest but I do know that five minutes after I was out of the event, I started driving north back to Ferrol. It was a big detour, it was not on the way to France and the next stop on tour. It simply happened, it was not planned at all.

Like the tractor beam from a death star it just sucked me north and back to Ferrol and the goddess.

I had never done this before, it was breaking from the plan. Of course, there was a plan and it was a simple one. Do not get married before thirty and before then, do as much naughty shit as legally possible. Europe had opened up a whole new avenue of adventure and there was a new one to be had every single week.

There is always that one random decision that changes your life forever.

I have been thinking about this a lot lately; are some things just destined do we actually control the outcomes of our lives or are some things just destined to happen no matter what we do. Can a series of apparently unrelated decisions lead you to a place you were always destined to be, or by constantly taking logical conscious actions can and do we actually own and control our destiny. A bit of both is most probably the answer, but sometimes shit just happens.

My split second random decision came on the A1 heading north towards O Porto. I had moved into the exit lane, put on the indicator to take the exit east and towards France and the future that was carefully set out for me.

I looked at the sign, and when it came to turn the wheel to head off the highway, my arms just did not move. I just drove straight past it towards my new destiny.

VII
"INTO THE BLUE AGAIN AFTER THE MONEY'S GONE"

If you have ever had an anaesthetist standing over you, dressed in that horrible green gown, mouth and nose covered in a mask, eyes hidden behind glasses, you will know how terrifying that is. The brightest of lights a terrifying pod of impossibly bright, round lights, blinding you. When the anaesthetist leans over, placing you in their shadow, haloed in that eerie white light, syringe in hand, and they say, "please count back from ten". That is a truly terrifying moment.

10 - 9 - 8 - 7

Gone!

I have a dislike of hospitals. I think I said that already. They strike fear into my very soul, but for some reason they also make me feel safe, they have saved me before. After fourteen days of uncertainty, I was going back under the knife.

My future hanging in the balance, just two weeks earlier, life's problems seemed insurmountable. Now they just simply seemed impossible. Nothing had changed, except now I had to face those seemingly insurmountable issues from a hospital bed and most probably a wheelchair for the rest of my life, and I was broke, dead broke.

It turns out my travel insurance and medical insurance would not be covering any of these costs. As a resident in Spain for the last fifteen years my insurance would not cover me in my country of birth for some reason. The fine print was clear as day, I would have full coverage in any country in the world, except Spain and South Africa. I was ruined, physically, emotionally, and now financially. I had worked so hard, against all the odds and in a second it was gone, all gone.

Dr Greef leaned over, gave me a fleeting smile and said, "it′s going to be ok, just relax". The anaesthetist, looking like some kind of white death-angel, leaned over blocking out the light and said, "just count back from ten"

VIII
"ONCE IN A LIFETIME"

10 – 9 – 8 – 7 - - - -

Gone!

I remembered the first time like it was yesterday, it´s deeply etched into my brain, a memory that has guided my life, the first of many real life changing experiences.

November 1973, Durban, South Africa I had just turned nine years old and had been given the single most important birthday present of all time, a seven foot second hand single fin "Holmes" surfboard. It was a pristine spring day on the Zululand coast, hot, sunny, not a cloud in the sky. We drove the fifty kilometres up the east coast from Durban to Ballito Bay where my Mom, my brother Troy who was two and step father Bruce used to go on Sunday mini road trips, to hang out on the beach, have a picnic while Bruce would surf with friends from the "Bay".

I grabbed my board and ran down the path to the beach, my skinny arms barely hanging onto my new treasure. I heard my mom shouting to be careful and to wait for them as she unloaded all the goodies for the picnic and struggled to get Troy out of the car. My mom's words were just a background noise as I saw the Indian Ocean sparkling green and blue before me as I broke through the bushes out onto the beach. Without a second thought I stripped off my shirt and ran headlong into the shore break, my surfboard under me, a small one – two foot swell running. It took me about thirty seconds to reach the little waves at the backline. At that precise moment my Mom, Bruce and Troy walked onto the beach. I turned and caught my very first wave. Thinking back, it's quite astounding that I had actually managed to stand up and ride that foamy wave all the way up the sand.

The moment when I looked up not quite realizing what had actually just happened and seeing the beaming smiles and look of amazement on the faces of my Mom and Bruce will live with me forever.

 A bolt of lightning did not strike me down, I did not know this was the single most defining moment in my young life just then, I just picked up my board turned around and ran straight back into the sea.

Three minutes later things were not quite as fun.

 A rip current had quickly formed and was swiftly pulling me out to sea. An old guy swam up to me and asked, "Are you ok", of course I said I was but I was terrified. My Mom and Bruce were setting up things on the beach and had not noticed I was going straight out to sea. There are a lot of rocks at Ballito Bay and I went from glory to fear in a matter of minutes. I put my head down and paddled for my life and managed to luckily get out of the rip current and make it to the beach. No one had even noticed, but for me that was enough for one day.

That November spring day I learnt two valuable life lessons.

Surfing was what I wanted to do, I had strived for my mother's attention, I saw by the look on her face that morning that by surfing, I might have that, after all Bruce surfed and she certainly loved him.

The other lesson, I could have heeded a little more.

Never underestimate the power of the ocean.

That second lesson would be a recurring one that has continually conditioned my life.

In a matter of minutes my life was changed forever. Almost every decision I have ever taken since that day has been a direct consequence of those ten minutes on the beach at Ballito Bay way back in November 1973.

I went to the beach a young boy.

I came home that day a surfer and things would never quite be the same again.

IX
"AND YOU MAY ASK YOURSELF, WELL HOW DID I GET HERE"

It took a few years after that first day in Ballito before I started surfing with my friends Wade and Paw-Paw. We would go down to South Beach where the waves were smaller and a lot easier to surf, I had been given an amazing purple Lightning Bolt channel bottom single fin and it was my absolute pride and joy.

We lived on the Bluff and the waves there were way too heavy for us at first and the older locals were also a wild bunch and they scared the hell out of us. So, the first few years we would go into "Town" early in the morning and learn to surf by ourselves. My Mom, Troy and Bruce lived in town pretty near the beach so it made things really easy. We would get a lift into town spend the morning at south beach, surfing and just hanging out.

They were amazing times, there was no danger, the beaches were safe and we had everything one could possibly ask for. Soccer was still my main sport and surfing was just a pastime really. We lived on the beach and surfing was just something one did. Sport in those days was just that, sport. There was virtually no professional sport of any kind at all and believe it or not, any kind of organized sport on Sunday was not allowed by the Nationalist government. Sunday was a day of rest.

Not for a second did I ever think surfing would become such an important part of my life. I never set out with that goal in mind, it just kind of fell into place, one steady step at a time. On reflection, I sometimes feel it was just destined to be.

My uncle "Harry Hot Dog" was one of South Africa`s pioneer surfers, multi titled national champion and a surfing living legend.

Bruce was one of the men at the Bay of Plenty, the spawning ground of South African surfing talent.

And last but by far the most important piece in this equation was, I lived just a few hundred metres from "Garvies Beach" on the Bluff.

"Garvies Beach", one of the most localized beaches in Durban and one of the best beach breaks in South Africa.

We grew up without television which only came later to South Africa. On the weekends, I would wake up before dawn and walk down to Wade`s house and his older brothers or dad would drive the twenty kilometres into town and South Beach. We were so surf stoked we would paddle out before the first light of dawn and sit at backline in the pitch dark. The only way we could tell if a wave was coming, was when the horizon, which was always lit up with the cargo ships that were always at anchor awaiting entry into Durban harbor, suddenly went black. That meant a wave was coming and we would turn and paddle. Once the wave started to stand up it would catch the reflection of the lights from the many buildings along the shoreline and we would be able to surf in that semi dark dawn light. We had no wetsuits, no leashes, none of the equipment the young kids have nowadays. Our first leashes were a length of surgical rubber with a sock tied to one end which we then tied to our ankles. Surf shops did not even exist then.

For breakfast we would run to the bakery and get the reject donuts, Chelsea buns and bread that had just come out of the ovens but had small defects so they were sold to us for almost nothing at the back entrance.

I soon got bored by the waves at South Beach as they were soft and easy to surf. The next spot north was the Wedge. I loved the Wedge, good surfers hung out there. It was a very shallow reef break that broke up close to the old wooden pier. I loved the left that came off the reef and I soon ended up surfing there more than anywhere else. Even though Bruce was always up at the Bay, I was nervous to go there, all of South Africa's best surfers hung out there and I needed to get a lot better before I dared paddle out at the "Bay Bowl".

One man ruled the Wedge, he pretty much ruled everywhere but he was the undisputed king at the Wedge and he took no shit from anyone. Every wave was his and he ripped, we all wanted to be like him. Espo was the king.

The old wooden pier was an excellent fishing spot and it was always full of fisherman, fishing for Shad, Grunter and Pompano on the Wedge reef. This inevitably led to drama as they would cast their sinkers and hooks right into the middle of the tightly packed bunch of surfers, surfing on the reef. Surfers and fisherman have always had a love hate relationship on the Durban piers.

It was in 1981 when everything changed forever. I had finally made the change to the "Bay Bowl" and started hanging out at Dante`s Milk Bar, watching the best surfers in South Africa every second weekend when I spent time at my Mom`s house which was just a very short walk away.

We had gone to Jeffreys Bay for the first time in summer of 1981 and I had shared the line up at Seal Point with Simsy and Rustin, both of whom were standouts for the Natal provincial junior surfing team. That trip was one of the best holidays I had ever been on. It really was love at first sight. That summer a fire was lit in my soul which still burns bright to this day.

"Pottz" also surfed at South Beach before he surfed the Bay. He was just another one of the guys who absolutely ripped in Durban. There were a lot of unbelievable surfers around at all of the town beaches. It was obvious "Pottz" was an amazing talent but so were so many other young surfers, "Tucker", "Burn", "Hooded",

"Spowy", "Toast" the list of red hot surfers was long.

I never at the time realized how high the standard of surfing in Durban really was. We were so isolated from the rest of the world down on the southern tip of Africa and we only ever got to see other international surfers when the pro tour circus came to town for the Gunston 500.

The tour surfers were like gods, I had their photos plastered all over the walls in my bedroom, every centimetre of wall had cut up surfing magazine pages of the world's best surfers staring down at me twenty four hours a day. I would lie in bed and dream of surfing those exotic waves that every now and again we would see when a surf movie would come to town and be shown at the Jewish Club. We would go at least twice to see the same movie in order to absorb everything.

Hawaii, Australia, Indonesia, Tahiti, Fiji, places you could only dream about would spring to life on the big screen, they were truly magical nights.

The Gunston 500 was a big event in Durban, thousands of people would flock to the beach every day to watch the contest which was held in July, our winter school holidays. I would go down every day and I would watch every single heat, it was the greatest show on earth, I would go and just suck in as much as I could.

"Pottz" had just beaten Shaun Tomson, who was and remains South Africa´s only world champion. In his very first event as a pro the week before the Gunston 500 in East London he went on a rampage that July which to this day is unequalled in the history of the ASP and professional surfing. He was fifteen years old and in his very first professional world tour event, he destroyed everyone on his way to the final. "MR" the reigning world champ finally put an end to his charge. He then did exactly the same thing the very next week at the Mainstay world tour event and lost the final to the world number two, Cheyne Horan.

He was just another one of the crew at the beach and at only fifteen years old had just come second twice in a row in his very first two pro world tour events.

I had sat on the roof of Newton's in awe and watched every single minute, it was one of the most amazing things I had ever seen. 1981 was a big year for lighting fires in my gut that's for sure.

If we put what happened those two weeks in Durban into perspective it is just mind blowing really. A fifteen year old kid from your local beach, enters your local pro world tour event, via the trials, makes the main event, and wins every single heat and only loses to Kelly Slater in the final. Absolutely amazing!!!! Then the very next week he does exactly the same thing and loses to John John in the final. Well that's what happened. It happened right before my eyes and it will never ever, ever happen again.

I had never ever surfed in a competition before that week, that changed right there and then. Surfing was a school sport and I decided that I would begin to compete. At school we had to play two sports a year; a winter sport and a summer sport. Rugby was compulsory, we had to play rugby in winter, so I decided surfing would be my summer sport. We had our school surfing competitions at Anstey's beach every Saturday morning.

I did not surf at Ansteys but a kilometer up the beach at Garvies. We had a good friendly rivalry at school between our beaches, no one had ever beaten the guys from Anstey`s, ever. Our school has a great surfing history with Spider, Arthur, Rudi, the Spowy brothers and Brad all having surfed for the South African national team and they all came from Anstey`s Beach.

By 1982 I had a magically good surfboard, "Air Force One", a Spider Murphy shaped twin-fin, I was the high school surfing champion and Garvies Beach had gained total domination of the Grosvenor Boys High School surfing bragging rights. I was starting to get a craving for that heady feeling of winning.

"The Bluff"

If you ask someone from the Bluff where they come from they will never, ever say they are from Durban, the answer will be the same every time "The Bluff" will be the answer.

"Rough and tough and you come from the Bluff", is normally the response.

To which your reply is a simple "Of Course". My family has lived on the Bluff for generations and it will always be home.

The Bluff is a narrow peninsular of land that sticks out into the Indian Ocean on the south side of the Durban harbour and clearly is in Durban. People from the Bluff don't consider themselves to be from Durban. We just feel that we are different, as of course we are.

"A breed apart on the other side of Durban"

There is pretty much only one way in and one way out to and from the Bluff and it has some of the best waves you can ever imagine, it holds the north east wind well which is a horrid, direct onshore, on the main Durban beaches. Localism at all the Bluff beaches has always been a thing and they have been fiercely protected for a long time. North to South the main beaches are Garvies, Anstey`s, Cave Rock, Brighton and Treasure, with plenty of empty breaks in between. It is an empty paradise of waves, fishing, diving and all the good important things in life. The ocean on the Bluff is never flat, it gets every bit of North and South swell the Indian Ocean can muster.

More than half the area of the Bluff is made up of a military area on the Northern end and was home to the elite "RECCE" divisions (Reconnaissance commando) of the "SADF" (South African Defense Force). I lived on the Northern side of the Bluff, my primary school was a few hundred metres away and the nearest beach to home was Garvies.

We all pretty much stated surfing Garvies at the same time, a kind of evolution from the safe waves of town to the rock and roll of the waves nearest to home. It was 79" or 80" when I finally got the courage to walk down Sloane Road with my little twin fin and face the local crew of older guys who ruled at Garvies.

We all did the same thing pretty much at the same time, so it made life a bit easier. Paw Paw, Wade, Wayne, Thomas, Leroy, Jack, Johan, Baffy, Tony, Brent. We were the new wave of kids who, all of a sudden, invaded the lineup.

It was kind of a safety in numbers thing, but we all had to pay the price. There was a heavy bunch of older locals and they made sure we learnt how things were going to be if we wanted to call Garvies our beach. Chippy, Wayne,

Brian, Rodney, Lance, Lofty and drunken Duncan all rode motorbikes, had panel vans, girlfriends, they charged hard, they had rules that absolutely needed to be obeyed and they made our lives hell.

> You would be buried in the sand as many times as need be and pissed on for any deemed offence.
> You could never paddle for any wave unless permission was previously granted.
> You had to go on any wave you were told to paddle for.
> You would be dragged naked around the car park for fun.
> You would not surf on the same side of the pipe unless invited.
> You would learn "If you don't live here, you do not surf here."
> You would make sure the "Town Clowns go home".
> You would respect your elders and obey their every wish.
> You would FREQUENTLY have dog shit smeared all over you.
> You would enjoy it and have fun or you would be punished.

That first summer I spent every single possible moment down at the beach, there are no shops, showers, toilets or anything down at Garvies and it was heaven. We would starve, dehydrate, get sunburned to a crisp and at the end of every day crawl up the steep hill and home as happy as you could possibly imagine.

They were the glory days and we knew our turn would come. Soon it would be our responsibility to uphold the tradition and keep our sanctuary safe from intrusion.

I don't think we ever imagined just how out of hand things would get.

Surfing had taken over. I honestly only thought about going surfing, about the weather, about technique, every spare second of my day was lost to surfing, it was bordering on obsession. School work started to suffer.

I would get dropped off at school every day by my dad at about a quarter to seven every morning, there were days when you just knew the surf was going to be going crazy. The autumn early mornings when the offshore was blowing, the sun was shining, the surf was pumping and not a single person was at the beach.

Those were the days when I would walk straight in the front gate at school, get a surf report from someone who had seen the waves as lot of my friends lived overlooking the beach and go up to Wade who was my main bunking partner. Not much had to be said, we would just keep walking and go straight out the back gate of school and head off home to steal our own surfboards and spend a day of paradise surfing, while everyone was at school.

Sounds too easy and actually it was, but there were consequences. "Bunking" school was punished with "SIX OF THE BEST", a brutal caning from the headmaster. Six lashes that would leave your backside battered, bruised and bleeding.

We knew, the rules were clear, there was no grey area.

If you got caught you would be severely whipped and you would walk around in pain for a few days. You would be punished at school and then again at home. Six of the best was not something to be taken lightly. It was pain, severe pain. No matter how hard you tried to hold the tears back after the third or fourth stroke of the cane, they were the killer blows, the ones that broke the skin and started the bleeding, tears welled.

Mr. Evans, the headmaster,r was not an absolute psychotic maniac, he would always let you regain your composure and wipe away the tears before you left his office to face your school friends. They were always listening and waiting with evil sadistic glee.

We knew the consequences, so we would always take the back roads first to Wade´s house to pick up his surfboard then to my house to get mine. The Bluff was like living with one huge extended family everyone knew everyone, so if one of you parent`s friends saw you sneaking around the streets in school hours it would not take long before you were in trouble, so we took the longer route, the back roads to make sure we were not caught.

Wade`s mom was always home so we always had some amazing story to tell in order to explain why we were back home from school so early. Our favourite was we collected so many newspapers that month for recycling we got the day off. I guess I will never know if she actually believed us, but she always just smiled and said that was wonderful and gave Wade his packet of Simba chips and off we went, onwards to my house.

No one was at my home except Gretta she lived in the ikhaya (Zulu meaning home) behind the garage and worked in the house full time, cleaning, cooking and basically running after us twenty four hours a day. She would not believe a word of what I was saying and would scold me but she would never ever give me up. Geez Gretta was a legend, funny how you only appreciate people when it´s too late sometimes. I miss Gretta and wish I could give her one last huge hug.

From my house it was a quick run up Bushlands Road, then down Marine Drive to Sloane Road and Garvies.

It was just Wade and I at Garvies all day, and it was glorious. Sometimes the teachers would come and look for us, but they mainly looked at Anstey`s, and we were never caught by a teacher at the beach. We were however, every now and again, turned in by someone. Mr. Owen, in frustration I guess, turned me in once. First thing in the morning the next day we would be told we were in trouble and would have to go down to the headmaster's office at the end of the day. Mr. Evans wanted to give us our medicine.

The waiting was the worst, knowing punishment and pain is imminent is not nice. We would try to pad our underpants with toilet paper, it never worked and the result of the whipping was always the same, pain, blood, bruising.

The life lesson was clear, if you do the crime, be willing to do the time.

Did we do it again, pleasure and pain, act and consequence?

Absolutely, many more times!

My first surfing injury was at Garvies. My surfboard "Airforce One" shot into the air at the end of a wave and came down swallow tail first onto my head one afternoon whilst surfing after school. Thomas was right next to me as my head opened up, like a ripe melon.

Head wounds bleed a lot.

He walked back home with me, blood streaming down my face, back and shoulders. We were staying in Admiral Road while our house was being renovated and Gretta almost had a heart attack when she saw me. I remember it perfectly, it was a Thursday afternoon, and my dad was down at the Bluff Athletic Club and came home late that night, I sat in the kitchen waiting for him to come home as he was the only one who could take me to the hospital. By the time he finally got home a few hours had passed and the bleeding had eventually stopped. He took one look at the cut, shaved a big bald patch on the top of my head, pushed the cut closed and stuck it together with a piece of tape. First aid 101, if you can fix it yourself, why bother with a doctor.

The next morning, I was caned for coming to school with a non-regulation haircut.

We literally lived at the beach by now. We surfed before school which meant waking up at 4am every morning, going to Rob´s house, climbing up the gutter pipes onto the ledge that went around the house on the first floor, climbing along, past his sister´s bedroom, to his bedroom and then waking him up. We had this thing that we had to be in the water before the very first rays of the sun rose above the horizon. If the sun touched us before we were in the ocean we would turn into stone, so we would sprint down to Garvies, surf then be back home before 6.30am and then go to school.

Of course, if the surf had been absolutely pumping, like the one morning I can remember

where there was a slight oily shine in the water,
I would get Wade and walk straight out the
back gate and back down to the beach.

On weekends we would sleep on the beach, no
sleeping bags, just on the sand with a blanket
around the fire, not a care in the world. Like all
good things, those days were fast coming to an
end.

The Garvies pipe was everything to us, our
symbol, our rock, never changing, always there.
It saw it all, I once even managed to convince
both Super Moo and Minnie Mouse they both
needed to see the marvels that were in store for
them up the pipe. It witnessed Thomas ride his
racing bike off the end into the high spring tide
shore break. He did not make it and smashed
into the rocks. We were standing on it one fine
dawn morning when Lofty drove down onto the
beach with his XT 500, we were still just kids
and he waxed up his board in front of us,
walked down onto the beach swearing and
proceeded to beat the living daylights out of
every single fisherman on the beach before
paddling out still swearing like a mad man. It
watched as they tore up our car park and tried to

build twenty one duplex houses on our beach. We painted it in huge big white letters

"Don't Live Here, Don't Surf Here"

It watched us grow from young kids into men. It watched us go from learning to stand on our surfboards to getting barreled off our heads. It watched us fight, it watched us love. It saw it all.

It stands there today unchanged, our symbol, our rock, never changing, always there.

X
"AND YOU MAY ASK YOURSELF HOW DO I WORK THIS?"

At the time we did not know it was the beginning of the end.

It was still pitch dark when I walked down to Wade`s house with my board, the south west wind was blowing and we were going to watch the rugby and then go into town for a surf.

The "Springboks" the national rugby team, were on tour in New Zealand, it was a strong team and they were going to win the test series, which was something deemed impossible. To beat the "All Blacks" in New Zealand was an impossible task. It was tied at one test match each. The Springbok team was amazing, unbeatable, maybe the best team of "Springboks" ever assembled.

We sat there early in the morning dumbfounded at what we were seeing, flour bombs, rioting, and a ridiculous last-minute penalty that won the test series for the New Zealand "All Blacks".

When the game ended we went into town and surfed, to lose like that hurt. Rugby was a big thing for us and the Springbok rugby team was our country's pride and joy. Not in our wildest dreams could we imagine that morning we would not see the Springboks play again for another decade.

Politics and sport were as of that moment joined hand in hand. International sanctions against the South African Apartheid system were now in full effect. That morning was the first time I ever realized something was amiss.

Later in life this would have a profound effect on me along with all of the other South African sportsmen who wanted to compete on the international stage.

1981 was a big year that is for sure.

The summer of 1980/81, we went to Jeffreys Bay for the very first time. It's a long drive south from Durban to Jeffreys Bay, one thousand kilometres and eleven hours in the back seat with Troy in the Ford Cortina 3000 station wagon.

It's a good drive, down the Natal south coast to Port Shepstone then up into the Natal highlands and Kokstad and into the Transkei, to Umtata.

That bit of the journey, I had done a thousand times before, while going camping with my grandfather ever since I could remember. But the rest of the journey, onto East London, back inland to King Williamstown, down to the coast again seeing the Sundays River and the huge sand dunes just before Port Elizabeth and then that last anxious hour onto J bay, I had never done before.

The whole journey, Joe Jackson, The Police and Bob Marley blared out of the tape deck speakers, as the majestic rural country side of the Eastern Cape province peeled off before my eyes. My excitement growing with every kilometre we got closer.

We stayed in St Francis Bay, right in the centre near the beach, in a big house for the two weeks we were there and only went into Jeffreys Bay a few days later.

The road from Humansdorp to St Francis was an unpaved dirt road and had the most amazing dips and humps on the last long stretch into Seal Point, like a huge roller coaster. Seal Point itself has hardly changed, the bay has a lot more houses but the actual last bit of road into and around Seal Point is exactly the same.

It was a stunning hot summer's day the very first time I saw her, we drove around the corner mid-morning, the south westerly offshore wind was blowing lightly and a set of waves was charging down the point. I got my first glimpse of perfection. It was high tide the water was emerald green, the white dunes of Cape Saint Francis gleaming across the bay was like seeing a dream come true right before my eyes.

We came around the corner and there she was in all her stunning glory, a set of waves rolled through from the outside point, the first wave barreled emerald green over full stop rock, then hit the inside section and just raced off into the distance towards the sandy beach.

Simsy, Rustin, Bill and Kay were all there that summer, they were all top surfers who had competed in the South African surfing championships. I felt at ease in the lineup with them as they encouraged me to compete, to come into town and try my hand at the Natal monthly competitions. A few months after watching "Pottz" do the impossible at the Gunston 500, I finally made up my mind.

That summer at Seal Point, the seed was planted unknowingly. It was planted deep in my soul, a love for the natural beauty of the Eastern Cape and Jeffreys Bay. Unconsciously almost everything I have done since that moment in 1980, has led me back to Jeffreys Bay time and time again.

You know when its love at first sight.

A long distance love affair, an everlasting love against all the odds that has ultimately resulted in me lying tied to a hospital bed, my fate once again, in the hands of the doctors.

XI
"WATER DISSOLVING AND WATER REMOVING"

I am not sure exactly how we managed to scam our way back to J Bay only six months later.

Rob, Gavin and I alone in J bay for two weeks! We were only sixteen and we managed to get there, look after ourselves and surf ourselves to death.

To cut a long story short we managed to convince our biology school teacher, Mr. Owen, to take us to J Bay during the three weeks winter school holidays in July. Mr. Owen at best was a dodgy character and he would have loved to fondle my bottom. This we all knew.

I had learnt quickly, that sex gives you power, or in this case the desire he had to fondle my bum, gave me a hold over him. He also just happened to be the teacher in charge of the photography club which we of course all joined. He just loved the dark room and took a special interest in taking photos of me. With every photo he took we got closer and closer to J Bay.

Just so we get this perfectly clear, Rob and Gavin were always near and Mr. Owen knew without the slightest shadow of a doubt, that if he so much as tried to touch anyone of us he would have his limbs broken.

However, like most devious dirty men his desire was just too much for him and he agreed to take us to J Bay.

It´s hard to imagine how J Bay was back then, it was really just a small little town, only the one hotel in the centre of town. There was a single house on the point, not one single back-packers, no accommodation anywhere at all, just the Savoy hotel, the Rondavels or the Caravan Park. There wasn´t even a supermarket, just Ungerer´s general store.

We stayed in the Rondavels, a small one room round hut, no heating, three rusty old beds, a small gas stove, no fridge, one small window and a very small kitchen. The toilets and cold shower were in an outbuilding.

This was home for the next weeks and it was paradise.

I have been kind of thinking about the whole Mr. Owen deal, pretty amazing really. Would I have allowed my son go off with some dodgy teacher for three weeks, even if he was just going to be supplying the lift and we were not actually going to be staying under the same roof?

Of course, I would, if he had friends the caliber of Rob and Gavin watching his back, and I knew my son was as mentally strong as I was, of course I would. Fuck sakes it's a trip to J bay. He would be okay.

Okay, so after saying that, Mr. Owen did not just drop us in J bay and bugger off, no he came around and did spend a night or two. He came to check to see if we were okay or so he said. We were stoked, the long walk down to Supers everyday was a pain and when he was around we could surf way more as having his car available was a bonus.

He always seemed to have his camera in his hands every time we were getting in and out of our wetsuits and it was always pointed at my arse for some reason. He also followed us into the showers at night and took photos of us showering, the dirty sod! We all knew what was going on and played the game to perfection, we still had two more years at school and two more trips to J bay in July to nurture.

This was my first real surf trip where we were free to do whatever we pleased, just Rob, Gavin and myself and we were good, we did nothing bad, nothing bad at all. It was the first and last surf trip with Rob where nothing bad happened, every single trip after that one just got progressively worse and worse.

We surfed all day, ate canned curry fish with rice, drank lots of alcohol and lit our farts. Man, what a sight to behold. Our diet was less than healthy and the curried fish rice and alcohol mix made for some atomic bomb farts and when you have atomic bomb farts and you are drunk and bored in a dark cold rondavel, you light those things up.

Jesus, to this day I have not seen anything like it (except of course that time at the Café Paris in France, when DH tried to launch a fire rocket from his derriere) luminous green jet fuel flames lighting up the room, kind of like the northern lights with a smelly kick.

I can´t say this was the best most classic trip ever, as it was not, but it was the first and it was awesome, the first is always something you remember.

There was never really any doubt, that at just sixteen we would be okay. Honestly, I can't even remember if we had any money, obviously we did, but not a cash card that daddy would have topped up and we could just take what we wanted. No, it was nothing like that, we had a bit of cash and it had to last.

Fuck we had a good time, not even Mr. Owen trying to kiss me made Rob and Gavin bash him senseless, we knew he was our pass to more trips and our lift to surf at Seal Point and much, much, more.

While we were there we saw the very first Pro surfing event in J Bay the Beach Hotel surf Classic, I just knew right there and then I wanted to surf in that contest, even though Supers on my twin-fin was a nightmare. I just could not surf the place properly, I had no drive and the never ending walls of water, were just so different from the short, drop and barrel of the Bluff, I had a hard time surfing Super Tubes for years, but in the end I eventually paid my dues and got its number.

I know now there is no other place on the planet quite like Jeffreys Bay, where "Speed is everything". A lot later in life while on the world tour, Jack Shipley the founder of the Pipe Masters and Lightning Bolt surfboards pulled me aside and said to me, "Son, speed is a manouevre in itself" and believe me at Super

Tubes you can surf faster than anywhere else on earth. I had to surf the left-hand point breaks in Spain and Indonesia first, before I could come back and surf "Super Tubes" properly.

If nothing else, in writing this tale it has made me realize, I have done and or been involved in some crazy stuff in my lifetime. I am not quite sure how I am still alive to tell this tale, but it sure has been a fun ride.

It was our next trip to J Bay that we really lit the wick to everything that was going to follow.

We were now seventeen, had made our first trip and had survived. Mr. Owen was still around and he took us back the next year, but no Gavin. It was Birdman who came along this time.

Even Rob is not sure if this tale should be told. There are a lot of things I am not exactly proud of doing and this is one of those times but fuck, it certainly was amusing at the time.

It involves 8mm film, a cassette tape, two lady friends, Rob, Birdman and me. We most probably have done a lot of stuff we should have gone to jail for. No doubt, this story would have made a top three podium finish!

Of all the naughty shit we did as school kids, this was by far the naughtiest.

I loved school and could never understand the guys who hated it. I saw as clear as day they were going to be the best years of our lives. Well at least at the time I thought that. I now know the best years of my life have pretty much been every single one, anyway I digress.

School was always easy, I never ever made a real effort, the objective was to pass and move on. I just learnt the rules and got on with it, no stress, do what needed to be done. I worked it out real early in life, you just have to play the cards you get dealt, you either play them smart and win, even with a bad hand, or be an idiot and lose with three aces. I got dealt an ace and I have played it all my life, it's the other cards that keep changing as life moves on, but that one ace I have always had up my sleeve.

I knew I had to get the most out of my school days, after school came the army and a job, how the hell could that be better than school. I understood that clear as day, all I wanted to do was surf and hang out with my girl on the onshore days. I knew I had to get the teachers on my side.

Mr. Owen well that was under control, a few photos here and there, trips to J Bay and never a bad result in any of my science or biology exams. History was also under control as Duncan was the teacher in charge of the school surfing team of which I was the captain. He knew if I failed History I would be banned from surfing by my dad, so no matter how badly my History exams went Duncan always found a way to pass me. At the time, I never realized how those classes of history would mould my thoughts and ultimately, my future.

"Those who do not learn history are doomed to repeat it"
George Santayana.

He drummed that into our young heads, we needed to understand our past history, so we could move forward with certainty. Duncan is a legend, blind as a bat and he loved surfing with us, but could never see the set waves coming so we would just quietly paddle away from him and watch him get caught inside, fuck it was funny stuff.

I loved English, actually I loved my English teacher way more, she was by far the sexiest woman at school and I loved her to bits, I always excelled at English.

One night, on one of our many drunken nights out in town, Rob, Gavin and I, at my insistence, went to her flat on the beachfront, it was about one in the morning when I knocked on her door. Unfortunately, her husband answered the door and I made an idiot of myself.

I was young, only sixteen but I knew. "IF YOU DON'T BUY THE TICKET YOU WILL NEVER EVER CATCH THE BUS."

I guess what I am trying to say is, if you really want something you have to go and get it, just sitting there thinking about it is not going to do the job, you need to take the risk.

Of course, you get rejected, of course you fail, but if you don't even try, all those things are guaranteed.

We were at that stage in life where the limits were always going to be pushed, what was acceptable and what was not we had to work out for ourselves. It's a fine line sometimes.

The surf was the same, the rondavel was the same, the food was the same, the beers, vodka, cough mixture, marijuana were all the same. That year we brought along an 8mm movie camera, a cassette tape and girls into the equation and it got messy very fast.

The rest went pretty much to plan, a few nude photos for Mr. Owen, heaps of perfect waves and miraculously we stayed out of jail.

We met them opposite the funky church with the red candle that was always burning on the road going up towards the rondavels from the main street.

Dee was hot but Scarface was a bit of a bushy, we just walked past them on the road and asked them if they wanted to come back to our place, they smiled and said they would like that. We smiled, we would love that.

It was the middle of the day, the surf was junk and we had way too much time on our hands. Two teenage girls and three testosterone strung out guys were on a mission without any kind of supervision.

It can go either way really, a nice cup of tea and friendly chit chat, or an all out, no holds barred sexual frenzy. I'll give you one guess as to how this one turned out.

Birdman was on fire that day, just peak form. His one liners were all time.

Dee was keen, she made it painfully obvious. It was the first time I realized that there is some kind of fatal attraction being a guy coming from Durban and a surfer, especially to the Afrikaans girls in the smaller cities and towns. It was my first experience with girls in J Bay, it opened my eyes.

We contemplated making that cup of tea and debated what kind of pleasant chit chat we were going to have with these two ladies who, just a few minutes earlier, we had met walking past us on the street.

Birdman immediately gave the bushy friend the name Scarface. She had a small birthmark on her cheek and as she lit up a smoke, he set the tone for what was about to go down with this beauty and I quote.

"Scarface, I do not fuck ashtrays, so if you want to watch you can go outside and watch through the window"

It just went straight downhill from there. I have no excuse, we pushed things past the limit, of course we did.

She slammed the door shut as she left in a huff, it was one of those stable doors, like the one we had in the kitchen at home on the Bluff, with a top and bottom part. For some reason the top part did not stay closed and swung back open,

Scarface obviously did not want to watch through the window and just sat down on the steps with the door half open and listened to everything.

Dee just sat there on the bed making absolutely no sign of trying to get away, cool as a cucumber she sat there with a defiant stare. Kind of like okay, so here I am, what are you going to do about it?

We had only met her ten minutes before.

This was it, literally every single teenage guy's dream come true. A sexy slightly older girl just oozing sex defiantly.

There is always that moment when you actually have to deal with something you have imagined a million times before and believe me it never, ever, is how you expect it to be. No matter how many times you have played something over in your head, until you actually have to do it, you just do not know how you are going to react.

This was huge.

The next few minutes were just out of control, so funny, so exciting, so wrong.

I could recite every single word line for line but no ways in a million years is that going to happen, not here anyway.

I had this red blanket jacket, it wasn't mine it was Bruce's he had lent it to me, as we don't really have much cold weather clothing up in tropical Durban. So, he let me use his jacket to go down to J Bay in winter, it was just the coolest jacket ever, fur lined and a red tartan print. It was the best jacket I had ever had.

We were still somewhat wet behind the ears but we were not idiots, we knew you can't be having sex with some total stranger, she might fall pregnant, this was way before I had ever even heard of AIDS, so that was not a factor, we just knew you did not want to get a strange girl pregnant.

I guess that was what was going through Rob's mind as he got down to the short strokes and suddenly in a rush pulled out and tried to get to the open window to blow his load out into the garden. He did not make it and squirted all over Bruce's red jacket which was hanging on the bed post. I am not sure if it was the noise Dee had been making, as she was kicking up a bit of a fuss, or it was just by chance but right at that moment Mrs. Spowart, the manager of the caravan park, was walking past our rondavel and looked straight into Rob´s eyes as he stood there naked with his dick in his hand framed in the window. I suppose that should have worried me.

My biggest problem at the time was how I was going to get those semen stains off Bruce´s jacket. At the time I didn't blink an eye to the fact that we had some strange naked girl kicking and struggling on a rusty bed, her friend sitting having a smoke on the stairs outside, and an old lady looking at us through the bedroom window.

Bruce had a dark side to him, he had an aura that induced fear about him sometimes, I had seen him beat the shit of people. He had an awesome temper. Fuck, under absolutely no circumstances, could he ever find out Rob had ejaculated all over his jacket.

Bruce used to work selling top of the line suits, hand tailored works of art in the most important building of the time in the CBD in Durban, 320 West Street. If you have ever seen the movie "Kingsman" well, it was a shop just like that, called "Lord Louis". He would be dressed like he was going to the Queens ball, just absolutely immaculate.

I used to go hang out at "Lord Louis", it was just a cool place to be. One day, when I was about thirteen, across the building in the public toilets, a man tried to grab me and pull me into a toilet cubicle, I managed to break free and escape. I ran straight to Bruce and with a tremble in my voice and fear in my eyes told him what had just happened. He calmly picked up a wooden walking stick with a brass pommel from the hand of a mannequin in the window dressing, strode across the hall, kicked the public toilet door open and proceeded to beat the living daylights out of the fool who had not made a quick enough escape.

Bruce was an imposing man. I scrubbed and scrubbed that jacket clean.

Until that moment I always had this kind of ideal image of girls, they were just so perfect, they could never be bad, they could never do anything wrong, they just couldn't. Surely not!

Dee helped change that perception. Obviously, Cher had been a crazy little thing, but I kind of knew deep down she was not normal. Nice girls surely did not hitch their skirts and jump on you in the lounge while mom went off to make a cup of tea, I guessed that was not normal, or was it?!

Dee had opened up a whole new can of questions. Honestly, to this day, I am no nearer to any of the answers to the questions Dee started spinning around in my brain that day.

However, it did re enforce my ever increasing belief in my new theory. "If you don't try, you will never know". Rob, a few years later in the Savoy Hotel, put the final nail in that coffin when he just walked up to a group of girls sitting having a drink and without so much as a single previous word asked the one nearest to him. "Would you like to fuck?"

She looked up at him, then across the room at Gavin, Birdman and myself and said, "why not"

XII
"LETTING THE DAYS GO BY"

Pierre sat next to me in English class throughout high school, he lived about five hundred meters down the road and we were good friends.

His dad, Jerry, sold second hand cars in Durban. We all knew he had been a "soldier of fortune" and was one of "Mad Mike Hoare`s" right hand men. We had heard the stories of the revolution in the Belgian Congo and how romantic and adventurous it all sounded, but there again we often heard battle stories at school.

There was always some one`s older brother, cousin, or friend who was on the "Border" and every now and then we would see a few secretly taken photos of the guys up in Angola. The photos of a contact were by far the most eagerly shared, photos of bloated dead bodies of the enemy were the most prized.

The news spread though the school like wildfire, a commercial airliner had been high jacked and was going to land at Louis Botha, Durban International Airport. Our school was close to the airport and right under the flight path of any landing airplane when the south wind blew.

Within hours we heard the news on the radio, Pierre´s father was somehow involved.

To cut a long story short it went something like this, believe me I have tried to tell this story but no one believes a single word I say. And yes, this really did happen.

(On the 25th November 1981 a group of mercenaries under the leadership of "Mad Mike Hoare" were hired by the South African Government to overthrow the Seychelles government of Albert Rene. The objective of the coup was to bring down the Seychelles government of President France-Albert René and to re-install the former President James Mancham. René himself had ousted the former President Mancham in a 1977 coup.

Hoare and his forty three mercenaries were disguised as tourists, rugby players and members of a beer-drinking group called the "Ancient Order of Froth blowers." They arrived in a Royal Swazi jet on Mahé, carrying their own weapons. Nine mercenaries, members of Hoare's advance guard were already on the island on the evening of Wednesday, 25 November 1981.

"Mad Mike"Hoare, was an Irish mercenary soldier in the Congo living in South Africans a civilian. Among the fifty three people selected to carry out the coup, some members

of the SADF special forces (Recces), several former
Rhodesian soldiers and ex-Congo mercenaries.
The coup attempt was unexpectedly triggered off when an
alert customs official spotted an AK-47 assault rifle in the
luggage of one of the mercenaries. The invaders fought a
brief gun-battle at the airport and forty five mercenaries
escaped aboard an Air India jet (Air India Boeing aircraft
Flight 224) which happened to be on the tarmac and which
they hijacked. One mercenary died during the skirmish. Five
soldiers, a female accomplice and Martin Dolinchek were left
behind. The mercenaries took some hostages, who were later
freed unharmed. A police sergeant was wounded and an
army 2nd lieutenant David Antat was killed."

At the time this was exciting news, Pierre was
my friend, he sat right next to me every single
day. We had an inside track as to what was
going on.

However, and this has come back to me many
times over the years, I saw him every day and
what for all of us was just another adventure
story, for him and his family, this must have
been a living hell.

Pierre never showed any emotion, I actually
don't think any of us ever did. Deep down
inside we had been taught that emotion was a
sign of weakness and any weakness was and
would be instantly taken advantage of.

Pierre's dad had stayed behind, to fight a rearguard action, so his team could escape on the Air India jet. The stuff of legends, you honestly could not make this up. He was captured and sentenced to death.

I saw Pierre every day at school for two years while his dad was on death row. We went surfing, life went on.

I have thought about that a lot in the years since. I could not imagine my children having to deal with that, I honestly tremble at the thought of my children having to deal with something of that nature.

In a way Pierre is a hero, an example. A lot later in life, when I needed inspiration to get through tough times I have thought of Pierre and how hard that must have been.

Even though I had no idea at the time I was learning a lesson, no matter how bad things seem, keep the faith.

His dad eventually came home in 1983.

"The Seychelles Government arrested six men and one woman who remained on the Seychelles and the men were tried in June-July 1982. The charges against the woman were dropped. Four of the six were sentenced to death. After negotiations, all were eventually returned to SA in mid-1983. The South African Government, embarrassed, opened negotiations for the return of the six arrested men. South African eventually paid President René a ransom of three million dollars, of which his cabinet was not informed and came to a broader understanding with Pres. René personally. The Seychelles was of considerable strategic interest to the USA, USSR, France, South Africa and other countries, all of which sought to exercise influence in these islands.

After 1979 when SA's main supply of oil was threatened, Seychelles had a minor but distinct role to play in the new strategy of the 'total onslaught'. The islands offered potential military facilities and could possibly be used as a base for clandestine trading purposes in the face of economic sanctions.

Other reasons included landing rights for SAA aircraft and a strategic base on the important Cape sea route."

Oh !!! Yes of course, I think I forgot to tell you.

We were at war, a long, silent, futile war. Our very own African version of Vietnam.

"The South African Border War"

Also known as the Namibian War of Independence, and sometimes denoted in South Africa as the Angolan Bush War, was a largely asymmetric conflict that occurred in Namibia (then South West Africa), Zambia and Angola from 26 August 1966 to 21 March 1990. It was fought between the South African Defence Force (SADF) and the People's Liberation Army of Namibia (PLAN), an armed wing of the South West African People's Organisation. (SWAPO).

The South African Border War resulted in some of the largest battles on the African continent since World War II.

Following several decades of unsuccessful petitioning through the United Nations and the International Court of Justice for Namibian independence, SWAPO formed the PLAN in 1962 with material assistance from the Soviet Union, the People's Republic of China, and sympathetic African states such as Tanzania, Ghana, and Algeria.

Fighting broke out between PLAN and the South African authorities in August 1966. Between 1975 and 1988 the SADF staged massive conventional raids into Angola and Zambia to eliminate PLAN's forward operating bases. It also deployed specialist counter-insurgency units such as *Koevoet* and 32 Battalion trained to carry out external reconnaissance and track guerrilla movements.

South African tactics became increasingly aggressive as the conflict progressed. The SADF's incursions produced Angolan casualties and occasionally resulted in severe collateral damage to economic installations regarded as vital to the Angolan economy. Ostensibly to stop these raids, but also to disrupt the growing alliance between the SADF and the National Union for the Total Independence for Angola (UNITA), which the former was arming with captured PLAN equipment, the Soviet Union backed the People's Armed Forces of Liberation of Angola (FAPLA) through a large contingent of military advisors and up to four billion dollars' worth of modern defence technology in the 1980s.

Beginning in 1984, regular Angolan units under Soviet command were confident enough to confront the SADF. Their positions were also bolstered by thousands (approx. 250 000) of Cuban troops. The state of war between South Africa and Angola briefly ended with the short-lived Lusaka Accords, but resumed in August 1985 as both PLAN and UNITA took advantage of the ceasefire to intensify their own guerrilla activity, leading to a renewed phase of FAPLA combat operations culminating in the Battle of Cuito Cuanavale. The South African Border War was virtually ended by the Tripartite Accord, mediated by the United States, which committed to a withdrawal of Cuban and South African military personnel from Angola and South West Africa, respectively. PLAN launched its final guerrilla campaign in late March 1989.South West Africa received formal independence as the Republic of Namibia a year later, on 21 March 1990.

Despite being largely fought in neighbouring states, the South African Border War had a phenomenal cultural and political impact on South African society.

The country's apartheid government devoted considerable effort towards presenting the war as part of a containment programme against regional Soviet expansionism"

XIII
"AND YOU MAY FIND YOURSELF LIVING IN A SHOTGUN SHACK"

They knew how, the powers that be.

The programming had been going on for decades and we all happily went, no questions asked. The propaganda machine had been churning out the fear stories for as long as I can remember and they were true, all of them, or so we thought.

It had been hammered into our heads, the Russians were coming, slowly they were moving south down through Africa. Slowly they were going to conquer Africa, the "ROOI GEWAAR". The "Red Peril", the "Red Danger", was coming. Revolution was sweeping through Africa, Rhodesia, Mozambique and Angola were going up in flames, engulfed in civil war. South Africa was next, the war was on our doorstep.

Violence was a thing we grew up with, a means to an end. A way to protect your country, yourself, your possessions.

We all happily went, my father went, everyone went. We knew we were going to go. In one form or another we knew we would all give two years of our young lives to the protection of our country, our way of life. We knew we would be going to war. Not going was not really an option, you could choose not to go but six years in prison in Africa, is not really an option. You could of course leave the country, become an exile. Some took that road.

It was going to be the adventure of our lives and most of us were ready and eager. We first started wearing military uniforms when we were just thirteen years old at school. Every Friday we went to school in our military brown cadet uniforms and were trained by real soldiers for an hour every week for five years. We were ready and half trained by the time we received our service call up papers in the post. Some of us were just seventeen.

It was luck of the draw, you went where you were told. Some destinations were better than others, no one wanted to get an Infantry call up, no one wanted to be a foot soldier in the SADF (South African Defence Force) anything else except being sent to a SAI division (South African Infantry).

The day I went in August 1984, I was excited, I was ready and I absolutely wanted to go. I would do my bit, it was going to be the adventure of a lifetime.

It was also the last time I saw most of my lifetime school friends.

When I took off my uniform in June 1986, life had forever changed. Things could never ever be the same again. I had hoped things could go back to how they were but I had brought home a new friend and he was there to stay. He has never, ever gone away.

My nightmare is always the same and it never changes.

"I am in a tunnel underground, crawling away from the danger, the tunnel just keeps getting smaller and smaller, tighter and tighter and then it collapses. There is total darkness, dirt suffocating me, trapped and fighting for breath!" It never changes.

Military Service

In terms of the Defence Amendment Act (Act 103 of 1982) all white male citizens are liable to military service at the age of eighteen, and they remain liable for service until age fifty five. There are two intakes every year, one in February and one in August, and the majority of these new conscripts are allocated to the SA Army, the largest of the four arms of the service.

They are allocated to various bases and installations with their first ten weeks being devoted to basic training. This is followed by specialist instruction appropriate to the trainees' particular corps or unit.

After six to eleven months training they are posted to operational and other units and headquarters for the rest of their initial service of two years.
These conscript soldiers undergoing their initial two years military service are known as national servicemen, and counted as part of the Army's Full-time Force.

Training
Success in battle is dependent on well trained leaders and soldiers.
National servicemen receive their basic, individual and collective training at their respective units. In the Part-time Force training is done on a continuous or non-continuous basis with an annual maximum of twelve days in the Commandos and thirty days in the Citizen Force. Members in

the Counter-insurgency Force do their training in their respective commands whereas those in the Conventional Force are trained by their formation headquarters, normally at the Army Battle School at Lohatlha in the North Western Cape. This school with its huge training area and excellent facilities is ideal for all types of conventional exercises. Leaders and specialists of all ranks are trained at the respective corps schools. The SA Army College at Voortrekkerhoogte provides command and staff training for officers of the Permanent Force, Citizen Force and Commandos as well as qualifying courses for senior NCOs and warrant officers.

This is a copy of the letter that arrived in the post just after your seventeenth birthday.

As I said earlier, there were three choices:

Two years National Military Service

Six years jail time.

Indefinite exile.

XIV
"AND YOU MAY SAY TO YOURSELF, MY GOD WHAT HAVE I DONE"

I took the full force of the first impact. The metal panels of the vehicle smashed into my back, crushing and shattering three vertebrae. At first, I felt no pain, no fear, but I could see it clearly etched onto everyone else`s faces. I had heard the phrase "faces distorted in fear", now I instantly understood.

It was a Friday afternoon we were coming home, a weekend pass. Just minutes earlier we were all laughing, the boys had just smoked a big joint of Durban´s world famous "DBN Poison".

It was hot, as only a tropical summer hot can be, hot and humid. We were coming home, a few days back with family, a few days away from the reality of army life. I was the rookie in the group, I had only been at "121 Battalion" for three months and it had been an eye opener. Make no mistake basic training had been tough, but I had been fit and ready. Being in a frontline combat training unit was another thing all together, this was the real deal. We had already lost a Lieutenant just a few days earlier to friendly fire.

The next few minutes changed everything. I became another person, the same on the outside but inside everything changed, I would never go back, no, not now.

I know there are no answers to the questions I have asked myself countless times, I know this, but for some reason, I keep searching for the answers.

Why did he die and I live?

We were sitting right next to each other surely it should have been me? I was the one with the mortal injuries after that first initial impact. He was fine, just a broken arm. Why did Lieutenant Le Roux come to my aid and not his, he could have been moved much easier than me?

What were any of us even doing there, forced to be part of a war that served no purpose, against enemies that are now friends?

What are the odds on me having, just a week before, completed a first aid lifesaving course, which ultimately gave me the skills to take lifesaving instant decisions?

I know there are no answers. However, I still keep asking myself, why?

None of it will ever make any sense.

It all happened so fast. One minute we were happy, laughing on our way home. The next, broken, bleeding, and dying.

I had no idea what had happened, the impact threw me forward onto my hands and knees. I felt nothing but I could not breathe, all the air had been forced out of my lungs and I could not move at all.

I had never really been hurt before, little things, a broken arm, a few cuts, a few stitches, nothing drastic. I immediately knew this was different, I knew I was badly hurt. There was no pain, but I could see fear and terror in the faces of the people around me and for the first time I noticed everything was moving in slow motion, both sound and vision became stretched.

I was confused but at the same time everything was crystal clear. Lt Le Roux was there straight away, it was chaos but in the middle of the chaos he was there. For some reason we both just knew what to do.

I needed to breath, the feeling of being oxygen starved on dry land is not pleasant, but it did not worry me at the time. The look on Lt Le Roux´s face was way more worrying, he was looking at me, and I heard him swearing.

I finally managed to gasp a breath, with it came the first spears of pain and blood. I started coughing up blood and it was agony to breath, I knew that meant ribs and lungs but that wasn´t the problem, the searing pain came from my back.

I had my surfboard with me, a new Graham Smith three fin thruster, a relatively new revolutionary design, that day it saved my life. The first impact had been brutal but it was the second that was deadly, the second impact was the killer.

My surfboard was lying right next to me in the back of the truck. I was frozen and could not move, Lt Le Roux slowly managed to manouvre it under me, he used it like a stretcher and lifted me out of the truck and set me down on the road side.

I still was trying to assimilate what was going on, what had happened, how badly I was hurt, everything was moving so slowly. The moment I touched the floor, free from the truck and out of harm's way, that was when all hell broke loose.

The noise was terrifying, a huge bang, screeching, squealing, crunching, grinding, buckling metal as the whole messy mass of our vehicle somehow, as if by a magical force, miraculously only inches from my face moved up the road.

Waves of pain had begun to engulf me, I know I was moaning, but it was nothing compared to the screams of pain and panic that were about to start.

XV
"AND YOU MAY ASK YOURSELF, WHERE DOES THAT HIGHWAY GO TO"

It had started in August 1984 when I stepped onto the troop train and was shipped off to Pretoria for basic training in the SADF. (South African Defence Force)

I was eighteen years old, fit, and ready. However, I could never ever have been thoroughly prepared for that which would ensue.

We came from all over South Africa. Every white male over seventeen had to do his two years basic National Service. National military service was broken into a six months basic training, then depending on how things went, another six months further specialised training, followed by twelve months full active service.

Once you got that out of the way you were then eligible for up to three months a year call up for more retraining and active service until you were fifty five years old. The South African army and our training was one of the best in the world at least that is what we were told, and most were proud to be part of it.

We were all just thrown randomly together on that first day on arrival into basic training camp. Thirty soldiers per platoon, four platoons in a company. We had four companies doing basic training at our camp in Pretoria.

It was crazy, thinking back, thirty complete strangers from diverse backgrounds just thrown together under the control of a bunch of absolute lunatics, whose sole task was to break every individual down into someone who was willing to work together for the good of the group and was able to follow orders without question.

It was the first time in my life I actually had to deal with other Afrikaans kids. Apartheid did not just separate blacks from whites but English from Afrikaans as well. I went to an English school and Afrikaans kids went to Afrikaans schools. They were kind of the friendly enemy for us, the Afrikaans kids. "Boer War" memories still burned deep and for us the

English speakers in camp, there was little compassion.

I knew not one single person in our platoon.

It was a mad scramble to find someone with something in common to make an alliance with before we went into our bungalow and chose our bunk beds. It was easy actually us Durban guys grouped together, then the other English speaking guys. We were the minority, Wayno, Johnny and I were from Durban and we stuck together like glue.

There was only one other person from the Bluff in our training unit, Rudy and he was in another company. I had arrived fully prepared, I had shaved my hair off, a number one crew-cut. I was not going to let them have the pleasure of sitting me down and cutting my hair off, a kind of shedding of identity ritual. I was who I was and they would take nothing from me, or so I thought.

Wayno was my bunk partner and we stuck it out together, through thick and thin. He knew the ocean and was from Durban, there were no other surfers in our unit. I had never met him before that day, thirty plus years later, we are still the closest of friends.

It was almost surreal, I had already gained respect from some of the platoon just because I was from the Bluff, the Bluff's reputation certainly reached further than I had imagined. I knew it was going to take something special to get everyone else's respect.

Corporal Steinfaart was our instructor. He was a pretty good guy, just another young kid getting through his two years. It was the Sergeants and Sergeant Majors who were the heartless bastards. They were permanent army men, their mission was to make us ready to fight and die for our patria.

On reflexion, it's pretty horrifying to think they could actually kill 4% of us in training before any questions were asked, they were acceptable losses. From our platoon one of us could die in training in the next 6 months and not a single eyebrow would be raised.

Training was not that tough actually, I guess for the guys who were not fit and came from a softer lifestyle, it must have been hell, but the years of getting thrashed at Garvies and surfing everyday made it easier, for me, for sure. The tough part was all in the mind, the constant mental struggle. I had never been away from my family or the ocean for such a long time, the fact we were locked up away from everything and everyone we knew was definitely the hardest part. I quickly learnt to become invisible and to get through each day, one day at a time.

Never be the best and never be the worst was my rule, finish in the middle at everything, become invisible, never first, never last. Hide in plain sight. I knew I could have won some of the races and fitness tests if I wanted, I knew my time would come and when it did, I would be ready to take those fuckers down.

Never fight the system, use it, another life lesson burnt into my brain.

All of us had had an easy life, pretty much the best of everything. I know I did, I really thought it was normal, just the way it was. We had a live-in maid Gretta, she did everything at home. I had never washed the dishes, never washed my clothes, never made my bed and had most definitely never ever done any ironing before.

Basic training inspections were brutal, designed to break you, to break down your resistance slowly but surely. It was impossible to be one hundred percent perfect, Corporal Steinfaart would always find something wrong and would all be punished, no matter how hard we tried to get it right, we just never could.

Winters in Pretoria are cold, freezing cold with the high altitude and clear night skies the temperature drops into the below freezing zone every night. So, waking up at four am every morning to polish the floor, make the bed, iron our uniforms with absolute precision after only a few hours sleep every night, slowly but surely chipped away at our morale. The combination of extreme physical activity day after day combined with the lack of sleep and continued punishment broke a lot of guys. It seemed never ending soon it became a mission just getting through each day.

The isolation from everything was complete, no telephones, no contact with any friends or family only via written mail, no television, we did have a radio in our bungalow but that was it. I remember listening to the Olympic Games in Los Angeles. South Africa was banned from competing but Zola Budd was there running barefoot for Great Britain but we all knew she was South Africa`s great hope for a medal. On the last bend of the last lap she tripped and fell, even life´s small little pleasures seemed to be denied us.

Can you imagine sending your kids away to summer camp, knowing the monitors might just kill a couple of them and it would be acceptable, knowing they are going to be abused both mentally and physically, for months and months, until they are no longer the children you knew and they most probably never ever, will be the same ever again.

 No problem, no questions asked, it´s all for a good cause.

"FUCK NO, I DONT THINK SO."

Well folks, that is what actually did happen and no one seemed to question it even one iota. The night before I left, we all went out for our normal family Friday night meal out. I remember it like yesterday we went to the Chinese Restaurant in the 320 West Street building had a nice night out and the next day I jumped on the train and off I went, no big deal.

I guess propaganda can do that, the systematic programming of the whole country´s thought process. I know I did not even blink an eyelid, I knew that I was not going to be one of the statistics, there were way weaker kids than me, they would go first, I would be just fine. Or so I thought.

No one in our training intake died, the rumours were always floating around about the guy who committed suicide on the intake before ours in the showers, rumours of the guy who shot himself while standing guard one night.

It was the accidents that would be the culprit of most training deaths. Johnny put a bullet into the tree next to me one night while we were standing guard, it was freezing cold, we were shivering and bored stiff, the third hour was always the worst, a warm bed seemed still so far away. There was a real threat of being attacked on guard at night. The ANC (African National Congress) was very active by 1984, we were instructed on how to handle our weapons, handed live ammunition and sent out to defend our base camp during the freezing Pretoria winter nights.

Only Johnny knows why he cocked his rifle one night pointed it at me and pulled the trigger. The bullet thudded into the tree right next to my head. We were in big, big, big trouble. I got off as I was the one who got shot at, Johnny was not so lucky he got a solid chunk of time in DB (detention barracks).

"THIS IS MY RIFLE, THIS IS MY GUN"
"ONE IS FOR FIGHTING ONE IS FOR FUN"

If for some crazy reason you ever made the drastic mistake of calling your R1 rifle your gun, this would be your immediate punishment. While holding your rifle out in front of you with one arm you would have to grab your dick with the other hand and sing out this lovely little tune. Never would you be so silly as to confuse your penis and your rifle ever, ever, ever, again. Those R1´s weighed 4 kilograms and you could hold it for a while but it was always just a question of time before your arms tired and then you would be punished for being weak.

I first saw Wayno in the mad scramble to find a bunk mate on that first day of basic training, he was from Durban, blonde and we just seemed destined to be together. We never had issues we were there for each other one hundred percent. We cruised through those tough days, he was on the top bunk I had the bottom. We stuck together through thick and thin, we were untouchable.

Fate works in strange ways, we are friends for life, in six months we forged a bond that can never be broken and when we completed army we went our own ways, I did not see Wayno much as I was in Europe, but on the day I took the biggest emotional decision I ever made in

1993, ten years after we first met. After not seeing Wayno for years, he was the first person I saw, sitting on the wall at Snake Park beach.

Of all the people in the world to see that day at that exact moment it was Wayno.

He was the perfect person to have a chat to at such an important time. At that exact moment, it was him, who was just sitting there on the wall as if he had been divinely sent to be there to help me through those dramatic moments.

I had had just taken the single most important decision of my young life and Wayno was the first person to know.

I broke the week before. I suppose everyone has a breaking point. Once again it was oxygen, I could not breathe properly, my asthma was giving me hell, I had tried to hide it, but the high altitude, cold highveld air combined with the millions of Jacaranda trees in bloom in Pretoria meant it was a living hell for my lungs.

One morning I woke up and I could not breathe, every day was a hell by now and I just knew I was not going to make it. I did not hesitate, I asked Wayne to lock me in my Kas which was a small metal stand up cupboard about four foot high and two feet wide, I just managed to squeeze in, all squashed into a little ball.

Wayno just looked at me and did it, no questions asked. He locked the door with a padlock from the outside and left me there. I have always had a fear of small dark spaces, but my fear of not breathing was greater. At roll call Wayno told the corporal I had gone to the sick bay and that was it.

I squat motionless in the pitch dark in the smallest of spaces for about six hours before they came back and Wayno finally let me out. It had been a hell session that day, the platoon was dirty, sweaty and everyone was smashed, I had escaped, no one said a word.

I needed that day, it saved me. I recovered from the asthma attacks and regained my strength, when my chance came, there was no standing down, I took it with both hands.

"Toast", from the "Bay of Plenty " was a Springbok surfer and he arrived into our company a whole four weeks late. He had been competing somewhere and had been given permission to arrive late thereby missing the worst of training. It was then I realised sport gave you breaks in the SADF, if you were an "elite sportsman" doors opened.

The key moments in your life come and you don't even realise they are happening until maybe years later, they aren't planned they just appear right before you. You take them or you let them slip right by and that cold winter's morning in 84" it came out of nowhere.

 It was just like every other dreary horrible morning, early wake up call, prepare for inspection, deal with the whole process of inspection then fall into ranks outside the platoon bungalow for more training, more mental and physical torture.

But no, that day was was different. The Regiment Sergeant Major was there and the whole company was on parade, something was going down, that was never a good thing.

He had a funny smiley grimace on his face, the Sergeant Major that is, as he stepped forward and broke the news.

It was regiment boxing night and volunteers were needed to fight for the company.

Now there is one rule you just do not break in the army which is never, never, ever, ever volunteer for anything, remain invisible, hidden in clear sight, but right there and then I did, with no hesitation, not a doubt.

I volunteered.

The moment I heard the words come out of his mouth, whoever fights for the company can have a free weekend pass, win or lose you can go home, I stepped forward. For fuck sakes, we would fight for fun. No reason at all needed back on the Bluff, how hard could this be, gloves, rules and a referee and only one person trying to hit you, way too easy. Of course, I would fight, for a few days back at the beach and two nights back home, home with my family. Of course I would fight, it was a no brainer.

For the briefest of moments Wayno was there with me, as we stepped out of line and into sight, but then he was gone back into rank and I was alone, not another single soul from our company had stepped forward. What had I done?

We would get slapped around at the beach when we were kids, there was always the odd scuffle at school, but the first real fight I ever saw was in the Margate hotel and it was hectic.

We were just young grommets when we travelled the two hundred kilometres down the south coast to Banana Beach to stay in the caravan park, surf and go into Margate and cause trouble every night. There were a lot of us all between fifteen and eighteen and all from Grosvenor Boys High school and we were all quite naughty. It wasn't long before we were banned from the caravan park and soon after the Margate hotel.

I honestly cannot remember how or why the fight started but it was always the same, Margate was packed to the seams with up country holiday makers and lots and lots of lovely Afrikaans girls and big Afrikaans guys who did not like the surfers running riot with their girls, even though the girls certainly liked us running riot with them.

I was never a fighter, I was there for the surf and the girls, Rob and Gavin were the fighters but they were still young apprentices then, the older guys like "Troll" were the heavy bastards and just frothed at the thought of a good fight to end off another day at the beach.

That night we destroyed the hotel, the fight got completely out of hand, way worse than any wild-west movie, bar fight scene. It was the first time I saw Rob in action, he must have been fifteen then and he was just on a mission, breaking bottles, chairs and tables on people´s heads, everyone was doing the same thing pretty much but Rob was on a special mission he was on another level, he was in a crazed frenzy.

It was then I realised, Rob was special.

That fight kind of set the tone for all the others that followed, it was always all or nothing. The police arrived, the bar was destroyed and somehow none of us were even hurt.

We were all rounded up and put into the back of the SAP (South African Police) van, in the cage at the back, I had heard about what was coming next. The police officers leave the spare tyre loose in the back then drive you all around for a few hours with the tyre bouncing around smashing into everyone, causing huge damage to everyone inside. They would then drive you miles away into the middle of nowhere and then just dump you there.

We were all fucked, it was going to be the tyre treatment or straight into the police station, get charged, our parents called and the real problems would begin. The van, the van, we all wanted the van, please no parents.

It was then that the "Troll" took charge and stepped forward as the oldest most responsible person in the group. He was drunk as a skunk and had been one of the main guilty culprits of the whole scene that had just gone down. He called out to the officer in charge and said in a very drunken slur.

"But OSSIFER we just came here for a nice quiet little fight and now look what's happened"

Troll went all in. "Do or die, all or nothing" straight out of the "Bluff rules" play book.

I was outweighed, out reached, out gunned by a mile. I was the smallest guy to volunteer by about twenty kilograms. I nearly did not get to fight that night, there was no one my size to fight, so I ended up fighting the next smallest guy, but he was huge compared to me, at least he seemed so at the time.

"Do or die, all or nothing", was how it was going to have to be.

It was a pretty big deal fight night. All the top brass officers were there in full dress uniforms, medals, ribbons, wives and girls dressed up. It was the whole shooting match. A full size pro ring was installed and it looked like something from a Don King fight night, it was awesome.

The walk down the aisle to the ring was just spectacular everyone in the hall was just roaring.

I fought first, the opening bout of the night. The troops in the hall were just going ape shit. I had "Greeny" in my corner. He was a black belt karate and a pro golfer, one of the few English speakers in our platoon. He ran me through a quick tactical lesson on ring combat, control the centre, keep moving, keep your hands up, keep jabbing, don't get caught on the ropes, way too much to remember, adrenaline was just pumping through my veins. I wanted to get it on, I wanted to do this, I was focused I was ready.

I kept staring the other guy down, he looked nervous, for some reason I was fine, no nerves at all. Fuck he was big.

Three minutes is a long time, in the ring three minutes is a very long time, an eternity. This was the real deal, the ref took us out into the middle told us to have a good clean fight, we touched gloves and it was on.

I took two clean jabs straight in the face before I could even react, I was shaken and only five seconds had gone by. Jesus, this was going to be a disaster. I shook it off and came forward, I was at least a whole glove length short of reach, he just held me away and kept getting through with sharp jabs.

This was hell, I was going to go down in the first round. I was taking a beating.

I dug deep and stepped into his defence and let rip into the body, head down I managed to get some solid shots into his solar plexus and kidney area. I could hear the air go out of his lungs and see him flinch as he doubled up.

It just came naturally, no premeditation at all. I head butted him with all my force and broke his nose clean. Blood poured from the cut and the referee just lost the plot and gave me a solid warning.

The playing field was now level. Surely, they never thought I was going to play by the rules. I had come here for a nice quiet fight and now look what had happened.

Three minutes lasts forever in the ring.

It's amazing actually, just try to move around with your arms up for three minutes. Forget the fact you are getting the shit smacked out of you from all sides. After the first few blows I promise you don't see them coming they just land and you hang on, you fight for breath and you hit back, your arms get heavier and heavier and you just hang on until the bell sounds, and that is only round one.

I honestly thought I was going to go down in that first round, but the head butt kept me in the fight, it won me time to recover, it kept him away from me, he could see the blood spurting from his face. The bell rang and I walked back to my corner.

"Greeny" was shouting at me in the corner, he's killing you, move, move, move, get inside fight inside, he's too strong to fight toe to toe, it all just blurred into a noise. I stared across the ring at him in his corner, he was a bit of a mess. Could I see a glint of fear in his eyes? I felt like I had just had a two wave hold down at Garvies and the sets just kept coming.

There is always a choice, turn and head for shore or dig deep and paddle back out. I knew what I had to do, endure three more never ending minutes. No headwear protection, no gum guards, just him me and our fists. I knew I was also a mess, my mouth was cut to ribbons, my gums and lips cut and bleeding, and he just came forward, never ending. I knew by then I would not go down he had lost the power in his punches, he was done. I felt stronger than him. I could still win this fight.

I needed to finish on my feet, it was all I concentrated on, the second round finished even and we went into the final and third round, we were both hanging on by the end and he could have gone down, I gave it everything I had, but he stayed up on his feet.

The final bell rung and we both stood there in the centre of the ring, the whole hall was going crazy, my platoon mates were just going bat shit loony, I was a mess, battered and bloody. The ref got the score cards and raised my opponent´s hand as the winner.

I had lost the fight on points. Those nine minutes were huge in my life. A random opportunity came from nowhere and I took it.

Things would never be the same after that.

XVI
"SAME AS IT EVER WAS"

The noise was terrifying, screeching, squealing, crunching, grinding, buckling metal as the whole messy mass of our vehicle somehow miraculously only inches from my face moved up the road, driven by some kind of terrible black magic.

Waves of pain had begun to engulf me, I know I was moaning, but it was nothing compared to the screams of pain and panic that were about to start.

I was lying face down in my own blood, coughing and spluttering to breathe, it was hard to see what was going on but I could see enough, I wanted to understand, it all happened so fast.

I became terrified when I realised his head was cut in half, as I watched helplessly from the floor I saw someone screaming in anguish as they tried to hold the two pieces in their hands, trying in vain to put them back in place. Blood and brains in slow motion, slowly seeped through fingers onto the floor in front of me.

To this day I feel ashamed of my reaction in that moment. I cried out, "leave him he´s dead, get me out of here, I´m alive." I was evacuated first, Lt Le Roux got me out of there.

I never saw any of those people ever again.

I could never be the same person again. Fear forces change, fear and pain force change.

It took eight long hours before I made it to the hospital. The longest hours of my life and I´ve had a few long days believe me, but those were by far the worst.

I heard the words that spawned the fear after about an hour. I was still hanging onto my surfboard as if my life depended on it when the doctor walked in after the first brief medical diagnosis and blurted out. "Sorry son not much we can do for you here, we need to get you to a proper hospital as soon as possible. You have broken your back, it is a very bad fracture dislocation"

The next hours were hell and I guess I will never know why I was not given anything for the pain. I lay face down while my brain raced in a million directions and the pain slowly ate away at my resistance.

It was everything the pain, it was a devouring pain, it left nothing untouched and it strangely made me a man, I never realised it then. Of course not, not then. It took years for me to realise it but now I know it was then.

Fear and pain, they create change.

I started to cry, not the howling blubbering cry, a silent sob. As if maybe, hopefully, the tears could stop the pain, but they did not. I thought a million thoughts and tried to will the pain away. I could feel my legs and toes, they hurt like hell, I could move my toes in my boots, I knew I could feel them. You know the stories you hear of people who lose limbs and still feel pain and itches and stuff, so I was confused and terrified, I could feel my toes, but was I just tripping, was the pain just making me cling onto a false hope. I now know those stories are real, you do feel a lost limb, it does hurt, it does haunt you, like some lost part of your soul. Years later I crushed and ripped the end of my right index finger off, believe me the bit that's gone, hurts me every fucking day.

 The pain was everything, I just closed my eyes, hung on and sobbed my eyes out, the longest eight hours of my life. I thought the most bizarre thoughts, I had a ball point pen in my

shirt top pocket, it was digging into my chest
the whole time and I remember thinking. I hope
it doesn't leak, ink stains are a bugger to
remove.

I suppose I arrived in the early hours of the
morning at the main hospital, the ambulance
drive had taken for ever. At last things started to
move. Things moved fast the moment they cut
my boots off. First, they slowly cut off my
bloody uniform then last my boots and socks.
The doctor in the emergency ward had read the
first initial report and had seen the injuries.
Obviously, I never got to see them myself but
apparently my lower back was black, bloated
and swollen. I heard someone comment "IT LOOKS
LIKE HIS BACK IS PREGNANT" The doctor was talking to me
all the time, I tried desperately to get my act
together, at last I was in hospital, drugs were
just a few moments away. He was pulling and
moving my feet asking questions, it was hard to
concentrate, the pain had won by now, I was
just a blubbering mess. He stuck a long needle
into my left foot, I felt it, it hurt, more pain
added to the constant pain, and I cried out.

Things moved fast after that.

I wish I could say my recovery was fast. It was
not.

The months in bed, the three surgeries, the pain, the agony of being face down in bed for thirty straight days without being able to move. The uncertainty of the future, it seemed endless, for some reason I was not afraid, I knew what the doctors were saying was not going to happen, deep down inside I just knew. Maybe I was just young and naive.

The first diagnosis was really bad, no walking, then after the successful surgeries it got better. No more sport and most definitely no more surfing. Dr Hammer was my surgeon he was good and he made a miracle happen. I had shattered three vertebrae, T11, T12 and L1, the worst possible place. Not only shattered but combined with a huge displacement, the spinal cord was stretched and ready to snap or be cut by one of the loose shards of bone floating around.

He opened me up shoulders to hips, put everything back in place did bone grafts and inserted two forty centimetre long stainless steel "Harrington rods" onto either side of my spine, wired them up, sewed me closed and that was it, bionic man for months until the bone had fused and re-grown and the rods could come out again.

If those eight hours had been long the next twelve months, become an eternity. The drugs helped but not nearly enough.

If the pain was bad before, it now was now turned up to another level. The drugs helped for half the time, but the last hour was agony, I would plead to have the needle and the instant relief, it felt so good. It felt too good.

Two weeks completely disappeared from my memory, the pain, the morphine, the fear. I can just remember the worst parts, the tears, the agony. Drowning on a sip of fruit juice, I could not move, I just had to breathe. A never ending life theme, lack of breath. I had to sit up to clear my lungs of the juice that was drowning me. As I did so the rods broke loose and ripped out. The pain was indescribable.

The next morning, I was back in surgery.

It's obvious the realisation that you are mortal, the time lying helpless in a hospital bed, the thoughts and fears of all that time in bed made me change, but it might have not have happened at all. Wounds heal and the body recovers, it's the mind that needs to heal and change.

My father gave me the single most important thing in my life, while I was lying there in bed.

I don't think he realised it then and I most certainly did not either until years later. It was a gift way ahead of its time. Long before sports psychology and mind power became fashion, this was back in 1985.

It was a master stroke, he just been given me a perfect storm for my brain to work out. I had all the ingredients, fear, pain and time. Along with a long, long uncertain future ahead of me. I was only twenty years old and my father had just given me the single most significant piece of knowledge I had ever been given. It opened my mind, it changed my world. By the time I finally got out of that bed and learnt to slowly walk again, I knew nothing would stop me achieving my goals in life.

What was the gift he gave me? A simple set of audio cassette tapes, "The Psychology of Winning" by Denis Waitley, one of the NASA lunar astronaut's motivational speakers.

Change is constant, we should never stop evolving, when we do we slowly die. Routine and our safe zone are killers. This I suddenly understood, at first like a bolt of lightning, then slowly and constantly over the last three decades since those dark days in that hospital bed.

Believe me I have experienced more than should be allowed, I truly have lived my small dreams. Those dreams also evolve and constantly change, short term achievable goals are the key and always have a plan.

"If you fail to plan, you plan to fail. By the time I got out of hospital, I knew what I wanted. At first, I had no idea what to do with this new information that was spinning around in my brain, everything had been so easy until then. I had never had to make an effort at anything. It was all way too easy.

Suddenly nothing was going to be easy, everyone was telling me what I could not do. I had always been good at sport, any sport really it just came naturally, but I had never made an effort to excel at anything, life was just too easy to have to try any harder. I just thought, why try hard if it's just given to you on a plate.

I loved surfing, this I knew, and it was now gone. Everyone insisted that I would never surf again.

I am not quite sure if this is a curse or blessing, but I do know one thing. I just hate it when someone tells me it cannot be done. I love surfing, it's a feeling impossible to describe. It is not a sport, it should never have become a sport, it is way more than that. It is a constant challenge, an escape into the ocean, away from the safety of land and normal life. It is a fight to dominate if even for a few seconds an indomitable force, a never-ending lesson in strength and humility. It is not a sport, it is way more than that.

By the time I left hospital I had a mission, I had focus. I was the only one who knew if it could be done or not. I really wish I could say that was that. I had a newfound focus, surfing was my mission and it was all fine, I recovered went on to fame and glory travelled the world for the next thirty years, met my dream woman, had the most amazing children and we lived happily ever after.

Well actually!!!!!!!!!!!!

XVII
"THERE IS WATER AT THE BOTTOM OF THE OCEAN"

"Mrrrrr Martiiiiiiiiiiin------"

"Mrr Maaaaaartin-----"

"Mr Martinnnn----"

"Hello, hello Mr Martin."

A blurry green shadow was talking to me. "It´s okay, the surgery was a success, you are in recovery, just a second I will go and call the doctor."

What, where was I, what´s going on. A thousand questions firing through my very confused brain. My tongue felt like a piece of shoe in my mouth. Why was I so, so thirsty?

Where was Lt Le Roux !!!!, was the goddess for real, is any of this real?

At that moment Dr Greef leaned over me and smiled. He lifted my hand and held it in front of my face and as he squeezed, he said "Mr Martin can you please squeeze my hand"

It all came back in that instant, yes, I was in St George's hospital, I had broken my neck, I was in surgery. Yes, squeeze your hand, of course. For an instant, icy fear gripped me again, what if nothing happened?

I was afraid to try.

"Squeeze Mr Martin, squeeze"

I stared up, the lights blinded me, always the bright lights, why was I so thirsty?

I squeezed.

I squeezed his hand as if my whole life depended on it, and it worked, my fingers reacted to my brain's message, at first it was a slow pulse a slow python like grip. Dr Greef smiled, a smile of personal satisfaction. He had gone his own route for me, against the other surgeons wishes, he had gone the extra mile for me.

He reached down and lifted my leg into the air, pushed my knee up towards my hip and again smiled and said, "Push me back".

I pushed, he moved, slowly at first but he moved, he smiled again. This time he literally beamed, it was contagious, I was in a hellish state of pain, thirst and confusion, but I smiled back. I had been here before, I could do this and I broke out into a smile, we looked at each other for a moment, both happy. Then he was gone.

The nurse came back and said. "Mr Martin please relax, we will be taking you back to the ward in a few minutes, Dr says you can go home in a few days, everything has been a success."

Fact and fiction, reality and illusion all mixed into a fog in my mind, what was real and what was not became a problem. It was the effect of the anaesthetic I imagine, just close your eyes and relax I thought. The worst was over, it would all work itself out.

Just close your eyes, it would work itself out.

XVIII
"UNDER THE ROCKS AND STONES,
THERE IS WATER UNDERGROUND"

I was face down on the floor, within sight of the "Plaza de Toros" and directly under the gaze of Hemingway. The years had flown by, years of discovery, I had found myself. I realized that life can be taken in a split second. I needed to live my dreams, not just dream them.

A fine mist of pink aerated blood was being sprayed all over us from the seven hundred kilogram Toro bravo's nose and mouth as he panted like the crazed beast he was, only inches from my face. He had just sent Bullo flying through the air, he had horned him in the leg near his knee. It was Bullo and I and this crazed hell bent death animal, it wanted to crush, spear and trample us into the ground.

It had been a long hard road to recovery, from being told I would never walk or surf again to at last being in Europe on tour, but this was real. The blood splattering onto my face was very real, the moans of Bullo on the floor next to me were very real. My dream was turning into another very real nightmare and I truly once again, felt fear and danger.

I felt the fear and it came flashing back.

Maurice had said to us just the day before, just before we got on the train, "People die running with those bulls, it´s not a game. If the second explosion is more than sixty seconds after the first, get out of there, do not do it" What did this cryptic message even mean?

The amount of people walking the streets, all dressed in white with red scarves and bandanas was just crazy, this had to be the biggest street party in Europe, if not the world, it was unbelievable.

The night before we had got drunk, very, very, drunk out of control drunk. Before I passed out in the street, in a gutter actually, I remember seeing Bullo stark naked, dick flying free, standing on a statue arms outstretched. Had someone slipped something into my drink again, no please not again. As I vomited, Bullo jumped. A leap of faith, he just jumped straight onto the crowd of startled onlookers. That was the last thing I saw or remembered of that first night in Pamplona.

The water from the fire hose woke me up, the streets were being cleared by fire men spraying the streets and sidewalks clean, of foreign debris, such as myself, readying them for the later running of the bulls. Bullo was not far away, we needed to get sober and ready for 8am. What were we doing up into the foothills of the Pyrenees mountains in Pamplona? SAN FERMINES, Hemingway knew why, he had told the world about this tradition and we wanted to see what the big deal was all about. We had no idea what to expect. Go, run, dodge bulls, too easy, right.

Wrong.

Bullo and I slowly walked the route from the finish, towards the start. "Buiders Arms", Rich and Millsy were also wandering the streets, they were not that hard to find in the growing crowd, we were the only ones wearing all black. Our black "Surfers from Hell" t-shirts standing out like beacons in the tide of red and white. Finally at the start of the route we stopped and sat down on the sidewalk, in view of the wooden stockade gates that held the bulls.

Bullo, Buiders Arms, Rich and Millsy were Australians so when the American body builders arrived it was literally like waving a red flag at bulls.

They had to be seen to be believed, tight stars and stripes jogging pants, star spangled banner tightly fitting vests and to top it off, yankee doodle dandy socks. Builders Arms was having none of it, they were body builders, that was obvious, muscles bulging under their tight-fitting circus outfits.

"Fucking Seppo Steroid Monsters" he blurted out before we had a chance to react.

That was it, we were going to have to fight these beasts in the street, my head hurt too much to be fighting anyone, how do I get myself into these situations, I asked myself. "You heard me you fucking seppo steroid monsters" Builder arms insisted.

Now "Seppo" is a word I had just recently learnt from my new Australian friends. As far as I could gather a "Seppo" is a shortened way of saying septic tank and of course septic tank happens to rhyme with Yank, so from that, we get "Yank, Yank, you Septic Tank" which, I assume, finally evolved down to just "Seppo", for short.

The "Seppo" bit just went straight over these guys` heads, it was the steroid monster part they were taking an exception to. Yes, now we were definitely going to have to fight these beasts. Why? I had such a headache.

Builders Arms did not flinch, not one little bit, none of us did, we just sat on the pavement watching these two clowns losing their marbles, it was hilarious. Then the impossible happened. They both got down on their stomach´s and started doing push ups in the middle of the road. No!!! surely not, this cannot be happening, but it was, their inflated torsos just pumped up even more, their clothes pressing muscles tighter and tighter.

Builders Arms just had enough, he stood up. OH !! shit here we go, fuck I hate fights.

The last fight I had, had got way too messy. Nearly a year ago to the day, in, yes you guessed it, Jeffreys Bay. Just two days before I decided to have a real shot at doing something with my surfing, just two days before turning professional, things got completely out of hand.

I picked Rob up and promised his dad we would be good, we were doing a runner to Jeffreys Bay, leaving a full week early to surf and just get away for a while before the 1989 Billabong-Country Feeling Surf Classic. By this time competitively speaking, things were just flying along, I had a string of good results in a few of the national competitions and had begun competing with relative success as an amateur on the South African professional tour. I finally had a sponsor and was making a bit of spare cash but due to my amateur athlete status it was kept in a trust fund and administered by the surfing authorities, something I will tell you right now, I did not like, not one little bit.

We had been given a free apartment to stay in at the "Beach Hotel Cabanas" near the beach, later in the week Troy, Lefty and the rest of the sponsored surfers in the team would be arriving.

It got messy the moment we walked in the front door. Rob had one look at the lounge room that had a small balcony that looked over the courtyard and onto the main road and said. "This will be the orgy room" he proceeded to move all the furniture into a corner and placed all the bed mattresses together on the floor. I knew then it was going to be a long week.

Spowy, Tucker and the Hooded arrived next, they were our neighbours at the Cabanas. Now they were by far the best surfers I had ever seen, especially Tucker. They were also especially naughty. They were naughty, naughty, mischievously naughty. If you were ever out with the Hooded or Tucker, you would have to keep your hands in your pockets as their favourite party trick was to sneak up behind you, stick their penis in your pocket and have a piss. Rob on the other hand was simply dangerously naughty, this was lining up to be a recipe for disaster.

Talking about recipes, the night we had to go into Port Elizabeth to collect Troy and Lefty from the airport, Rob had made dinner, a big pot of curry beans. Curry beans from hell, he had soaked the beans in vodka, to rehydrate them, not water. The stars had aligned, there was a party in Port Elizabeth and we were going to stop in for a while on the way to the airport. The vodka beans had taken effect as we filled the car to overflowing, Rob, Dino, The Doc, ET and myself all squashed into the small VW golf. Were was Troy and Lefty going to fit on the way back?

Destiny has a funny way of solving these unexpected little misjudgements.

The party was full of young students, most already as drunk as we were. It took about ten minutes before all hell broke loose. From across the crowded dance floor in the corner of my eye I saw someone twice the size of Rob, throw a punch aimed directly at his face, before I could react the big guy was down on the floor and more people were jumping into the fray. It was carnage, girls screaming, guys fighting, blood everywhere. By the time I got to Rob, more guys were on the floor, I grabbed him and pushed him towards the door and we ran.

We ran into the bushes outside and hid away from the masses hunting for us. They would never find us in the thick bush, we had just finished the army, trained in bush craft, so I made a wide circle back to go and fetch the car so we could get the hell out of there. Everything had happened in a flash, I had no idea what was going on, I just knew we had to get out of there, we were outnumbered at least twenty to one.

Rob got caught!!! I managed to get the car, drive back rally style to where I had left Rob. Somehow, he had been caught and was being beaten to a pulp by a mass of people. I saw ET rush in, I rushed in. It was a mission in futility, punches rained down from all angles, we just got smashed.

After a while the police arrived, we were arrested and taken away to the police station and Rob charged for GBH – (Grosvenor Boys High, nooooo, Grievous Bodily Harm.) I never ever found out what happened to ET, Dino and the Doc, that night. Rob and I were dragged off to the police station, the other guys I never saw again. Not never saw them again that night, I never saw them again, ever!!!.

I wish I could say that was it, we had a stupid fight for no idea why, we got the shit kicked out of us and we all went home. NO, not so lucky.

Honestly, while sitting in the charge office in the police station I still had no idea of what had happened. It all went so fast, it always does. One thing I have learnt, when bad shit happens, it is always in the blink of an eye, lightning fast and you are never ready.

Rob was covered in blood, face cut to ribbons, someone was trying to stitch a cut above his eye, when the guys who he had fought walked into the station. Rob, no hesitation, pushed the policeman back, took a flying leap over the charge office counter and punched the first guy in the face. All hell broke loose in the police station. Fuck, I had to go and fetch Troy and Leftie, I slowly crept towards the door, got into the car and drove to the airport.

While waiting, I called Rob´s father on a payphone in the airport, I had promised to keep it tidy, promised him we would be good. All I could say was. "Send lawyers, guns and money, the shit has hit the fan", no I didn't really say that, but it must have been something pretty close.

People were staring at me by this time, I was covered in blood, my clothes ripped to pieces. Troy and Leftie arrived, they looked at me in amazement, I glared back and said "just shut up and get in the fucking car "

Things were just as bizarre back at the Cabanas. The Hooded had climbed up onto a balcony and into an apartment, thinking Tucker would be in bed fast asleep. So, he silently edged up to the bedside and proceeded to urinate all over the extremely surprised couple who were by that time deep into pleasant dream mode.

As we arrived, still in a state of shock, back from our little journey to Port Elizabeth, the first thing we heard was someone scream **"WAT DIE FOK GAAN HIER AAN"** and the Hooded making a very hasty scramble down the side of the building. Strangely, this was the second time I had heard that shouted in anger that year.

Two days later, somehow, I had made the final day of the contest. I managed to get through heat after heat, there were a lot of the world's best professional surfers competing in Jeffreys Bay that year, the "Billabong-Country Feeling Classic" had become one of the best events in the world, everyone wanted to win that title. How I managed to do it, I have no idea. The beans, the fight, they were just the beginning to a week of chaos, girls and police.

The first thing I saw the next morning when I woke up was Rob, stark naked, standing on the balcony, in plain sight of everyone in the street, cut and bruised from the night earlier. He had a bag of clothes in his hand and he was shouting "Meat pig, if you don´t fuck, then fuck off". As he shouted, he threw a handful of the poor girl, who in his cut and bloodied state he had managed to entice back to our apartment, clothes out into the street. He was a man possessed.

Builders Arms walked up to the first steroid monster who was still on the floor doing push ups and said "you wanna arm wrestle".

BOOOOOOOOMMMM!!!!!!!!!

I hit the floor and nearly soiled my pants. A huge explosion right next to us, I hate loud bangs, they scare the hell out of me, too many bad memories. This time it was just a firework exploding. The signal to start running, the signal to tell everyone the first bulls would be leaving the holding pens. The crowd went crazy, people lined every balcony and window, throwing flowers into the street, deliriously cheering and shouting as the first bull came into sight.

I immediately was pushed and I slipped and fell on the still wet stone paving, there were so many people, too many people cramming into such a small space. Builders Arms and Seppo

Monster, who were actually still trying to arm wrestle were trampled by the crowd. The fear was contagious, the sounds of the bulls snorting, the sounds of their hooves pounding the paving, the sounds of the cheering, the sound of panic.

BOOOOOOMMM!!!

AHHHHHGGGGGGGGGGGGGGGG, down, down, get down, take cover.

Okay, okay, it's just another firework explosion, did I say how much I absolutely hate loud bangs.

Fuck, what was that thing Maurice told us yesterday.

XIX
"AND YOU MAY ASK YOURSELF, AM I RIGHT? AM I WRONG?"

The first bomb blast I ever heard was a few months before I went into the army.

It was a pristine, perfect, sunny morning, not a breath of wind and I was walking up Bushlands Road towards the beach when the sound hit. The shock wave of the blast had a clear path across the Durban harbour and hit us on the Bluff a few kilometres away, I could see the smoke from John Ross House in clear view from our house across the bay.

I wish I could say this was the first and last bomb blast I had to deal with but there were a lot more to come. The targeting of soft civilian targets had begun.

Two days before Christmas in 1985 a bomb was detonated in the crowded Sanlam shopping centre in Amanzimtoti, five deaths and forty injured was the final toll, the war finally was in the streets and it was definitely here to stay. It could hit anyone, anyplace, anytime.

The Magoo´s Bar, car bomb, I heard like it had gone off next door. In June 1986 down the road from Natal Command and extremely close to home a bomb was detonated at a bar we had been to a few times. Rob´s ex-girlfriend was there that night. Three young people were blown to bits and died, sixty nine more were injured. For both these attacks I was on duty in the Ops room. It was a bar full of young people having a good time out on a Friday night, it had targeted people just like me.

There were way worse bombings in other parts of the country but these three I was involved in, in one way or another. However, it was the fourth bomb that most affected me, the bomb that went off at my sister´s school while she was a student. My sister was just a young innocent fifteen year old girl, she was at that school, the violence was getting very close to home, too close. This was no war against the "Red Peril" there were no Russians here. No visible clear enemy. This was something entirely different. This was just plain crazy. Crazy men trying to massacre a school full of little girls.

I know my sister and I have tried to talk about this briefly, but it´s something no one really wants to talk about. No one really wants to talk about those days.

Try and imagine this scenario, just for a moment.

Imagine a whole school of young girls not missing a single class, not one single minute of school time. A bomb had just gone off at their school and two men had been blown into a million bits and pieces, their bloody remains splattered all over the place. Shattered glass everywhere, blood everywhere, police everywhere, school went on as normal. Life went on as normal, as if nothing out of the ordinary had happened at all.

No, I can't really imagine it either, not now, it just seems impossible.

I was on duty that morning in the "Ops Room" knowing my baby sister was there that day. It is a day I will not forget in a hurry. At the end of my shift of duty, I went home, my sister was sitting doing her homework. I said, "Hi", grabbed my surfboard and ran down to the beach and went surfing.

What fucking crazy times.

"Police with tracker dogs were on October 25 trying to trace a man accused of being one of three men who blew up a school in Durban. According to police, the other two bombers died in the blast. Parts of their bodies were found up to twenty metres from the point of explosion at Grosvenor Girls' High School. The bomb was believed to be a Soviet-made limpet mine. the school was to be used as a polling station in a whites-only by-election to be held on October 30"

"Zinto Cele" was twenty two years old when he was killed on October 24 1985 by a bomb that exploded prematurely. Cele was an Umkhonto we Sizwe member and formed part of Operation Butterfly, a large-scale MK underground operation in KwaZulu-Natal in the mid-1980s led by the present MEC for health in KwaZulu-Natal, Sibongiseni Dhlomo. The bomb also killed Cele's fellow MK combatant Mandlenkosi Israel Ndimande. MK operative Sibusiso Mazibuko was seriously injured in the explosion but survived and escaped

"The bomb was placed at Grosvenor Girls High and detonated prematurely. The school served as a polling station and was the venue at which Pik Botha (the then minister of foreign affairs) had addressed voters the previous day. Operation Butterfly was responsible for the 1985 bombing campaign in support of the internal resistance campaigns."

Like I said what "Fucking Crazy Times"

It`s kind of amazing how things work out. This was one of the things that really freaked me out.

I never said anything to anyone, ever, but deep down, this was a changing point. I guess it was then the seeds were sewn, real deep in the back of my brain. Never in my wildest dreams did I ever imagine one day leaving South Africa, leaving Durban and my family for good, but in the end, I did.

It was then I realised things were not right, what I was seeing every day was not right, something was very wrong.

I finally many years later did get my sister to say a few words about that day.

"Everyone was like, these fools blew themselves up. Actually, they said it in a much more disgusting way. Deflecting the possibility that in that final moment when they took stock of what they were about to do. My classroom was just a few metres from the bomb, it would have gone off at eight am, while we were standing outside in line for our morning assembly. The glass, I do remember, we found glass shards for months after that. In the strangest of places. It would have ripped me and over eight hundred other girls to shreds. I like to think in an unexpected moment of humanity they realised what they were about to do and made a clumsy human error, a simple mistake, knowing full well their deaths would mean way more to the struggle than taking our lives. I actually wrote a speech about this a few years back.

All the work I do now, is somehow a ripple down effect of this strange terrifying thing.
It´s always darkest just before the dawn."
"Tamlyn Martin "

We were a small family of friends on the Bluff, Johan was on duty that night as well and was rushed immediately to the site to contain and clean up the mess.

"I have photos of the guy that set the bomb at the girl´s school, that's after it detonated. We found his arm at the roundabout, about 50 metres from the school. Tony and I were on patrol that night."
"Johan"

I had never really thought about these things before, I had never even had the chance to see the truth. The press was controlled, the propaganda machine was well oiled and it worked just fine. No ways could I have had a realistic view on politics before then.

I believed what I saw, I believed what I read and heard.

What I deciphered and saw at night on duty was not what I saw in the press. It was then I realised things were not right.

Everyone just got on with things like nothing was going on, a few bombs here and there a few bits and pieces in the newspapers about unrest in the townships, but nothing too serious. What worried everyone was the fact we could not play international rugby or cricket against anyone anymore.

I just pushed it all to one side and concentrated on surfing well again, my back brace helped, it made it possible. Slowly but surely it came back. I started to compete again, slowly at first but soon surfing became my distraction from the reality of seeing the country slowly spiralling into chaos.

Honestly if I told you what really went on the next few months and years, you just would not believe a word I told you, so it's most probably best I don't even go there. They were mad, crazy, times that's for sure.

The boys down at Garvies were on a mission and they were not in the slightest bit scared to cause pain and damage to anyone who dared happen to be in their path. Anywhere else in the world or at any other time, we all would have been in big, big trouble but we just seemed invincible at the time, almost untouchable. No matter what we did it just went unpunished.

Meanwhile the surf just pumped, pretty much every day and I surfed more and more. We slept down at the beach at night we surfed before sunrise we did our duty and we took having fun to the limits of legal and way beyond.

When you go into the army you get a medical classification. 100 % fighting fit was G1-K1 and dead was G5.

After the months in hospital I was transferred back to a military sick bay in Durban to continue my recovery, I really hoped to be given a medical discharge and be sent home, I still had fourteen months to go, but once you are in the army they will never let you go. I went in ten months earlier with a G1-K1 perfectly healthy and left with a G4-K4 medical classification just one grade away from being dead!!!

I served the rest of my time at Natal Command in Durban.

This is the big mystery. How did I end up working in the heart of all the drama, in the middle of the "State of Emergency", the real tough times of the Zulu uprisings and the Magoo´s bombing?

How I found myself working in the central "Operations Room" with a "Top Secret" military clearance I will never know.

Things in South Africa were taking a turn for the worse the ANC (African National Congress) were more active than ever, bombs were going off everywhere, the townships were a hive of civil unrest, violence and action. The border war had come home to the cities and more and more violent civil unrest was right in the streets. More and more soldiers were being sent into the townships to keep the peace and to control the situation which was getting more and more out of hand every day.

I ended up in the middle of all the decision making and worked in the "OPS Room", decoding all the secret codes and messages between the top commands and regions during the "State of Emergency". I was directly under the command of the Brigadier in charge of the whole of Natal province's operational force.

What the hell were they thinking, all I wanted to do was get fit and go surfing, instead I was in a bunker stuck in the middle with a bunch of lunatics who decided every day, who was going to live and who was going to die. These were the dark years. South Africa was placed under a

"State of Emergency" which was basically Martial Law, which went something like this.

"Serious political violence was a prominent feature of South Africa from 1985 to 1989, as black townships became the focus of the struggle between anti-apartheid organisations and the Botha government. Throughout the 1980s, township people resisted apartheid by acting against the local issues that faced their particular communities. The focus of much of this resistance was against the local authorities and their leaders, who were seen to be supporting the government. By 1985, it had become the ANC's (African National Congress) aim to make black townships ungovernable by means of rent boycotts and other militant action. Numerous township councils were overthrown or collapsed, to be replaced by unofficial popular organisations, often led by militant youth. People's courts were set up, and residents accused of being government agents were dealt extreme and occasionally lethal punishment. Black town councillors and policemen, and sometimes their families, attacked with petrol bombs, beaten, and murdered by necklacing, where a burning tyre was placed around the victim's neck.

On 20 July 1985, State President P.W. Botha declared a State of Emergency in 36 magisterial districts. Areas affected were the Eastern Cape, and the PWV region ("Pretoria, Witwatersrand, Vereeniging"). Three months later the Western Cape was included as well. An increasing number of organisations were banned. Many individuals had restrictions such as house arrest imposed on them. During this state of emergency about 2,436 people were detained under the Internal Security Act. This act gave police and the military sweeping powers. The government could implement curfews controlling the movement of people. The president could rule by decree without referring to the constitution or to parliament. It became a criminal offence to threaten someone verbally or possess documents that the government perceived to be threatening. It was illegal to advise anyone to stay away from work or oppose the government. It was illegal, too, to disclose the name of anyone arrested under the State of Emergency until the government saw fit to release that name. People could face up to ten years' imprisonment for these offences. Detention without trial became a common feature of the government's reaction to growing civil unrest and by 1988, 30,000 people had been detained. Thousands were arrested and many were interrogated and tortured.

On 12 June 1986, four days before the ten-year anniversary of the Soweto uprising, the state of emergency was extended to cover the whole country. The government amended the Public Security Act, expanding its powers to include the right to declare "unrest" areas, allowing extraordinary measures to crush protests in these areas. Severe censorship of the press became a dominant tactic in the government's strategy and television cameras were banned from entering such areas. The state broadcaster, the South African Broadcasting Corporation (SABC) provided propaganda in support of the government. Media opposition to the system increased, supported by the growth of a pro-ANC underground press within South Africa.

The state of emergency continued until 1990, when it was lifted by State President F.W. de Klerk

I had to wear a back brace for a long time, it was big and went from my hips to my shoulders, it was custom made, moulded and fitted to exact size. I was obviously not allowed to surf. I can't quite remember how long it was before I just said, "fuck it" and paddled out into the ocean again with the brace on. Of course, it was at Garvies. Unfortunately, it was on a body board, I had never tried a body board before but the water just looked too good to be true and the waves way too fun to just sit on the pipe and watch. I just grabbed it and went. The body board was a mistake, I hurt myself right away, it was way too flexible, a surfboard would have been a much better option but the damage was done, it hurt too much, I just couldn't do it.

I am not even sure if the surgery cuts had healed closed yet, they were ugly at first, huge big welting scars, down the whole length of my back and another huge one on my hip where the bone had been scraped off. Honestly, I have no idea what I was thinking but I was back out there again, this time on a surfboard, it was just too good to ignore.

I have thought about this a lot in the past, what drove me to take such a huge risk for such a short term, moment of pleasure, was I just young and stupid?

Instant pleasure and everlasting pain, a lifelong curse!

The whole situation at Natal Command was just bizarre, I could not wear my full uniform (Browns) for months as the boots were too heavy, so I dressed in an officer's uniform but had no rank and worked in a "Top Secret" office where access was very restricted. I was treated like royalty as I had direct contact with the Brigadier in command, it was just crazy. I had access to all the "Top Secret" documents, I knew we had nuclear weapons, I knew we were dealing with the secret services of just about every nation in the western world. I knew way too much for just a guy who just wanted to go home and surf, but we were sworn to secrecy and I have never said a single word about what went down in that room and honestly, I am not even sure if I ever should. I got to decipher and decode all the "Top Secret" documents. Then I would just walk out the front gate, go home and go surfing. I had access to an absolute arsenal of weapons that were stored in the "Ops Room", it was crazy.

Meanwhile down at Garvies we were becoming untouchable.

It was these next months that made me hard, I realise this now. The army made me tough, it made me a man, it taught me pain, it taught me about death, but being in the Ops room made me cold, it hardened me. It was there and then, that the real ideological change in my mind was formed.

121 Battalion was just plain combat training, the enemy was clear, the objective obvious. In the "Ops Room" it was all politics, I soon learned the enemy could change at any time and you could be sold out by the politicians in an instant.

We (South AFrican Defense Force) secretly started training the Inkahta Freedom Party (IFP) members to fight for the SADF in the townships against the ANC (African National Congress) based supporters and in August 1985 the serious township unrest exploded in and around Durban. The rest of the white population had no idea what was going on, but every single day I deciphered the situation reports (SITREPS) and counted the casualties on both sides and watched as the command officers decided how long they would sit back and let the killing continue. Until one day they sent the troops in to clean up the mess.

In the mornings after doing the night shift, or the end of the day after a day shift, I would walk out the front gate, go home and just go surfing and I never said a word to a single soul.

No one knew what was really going on.

Somewhere, somehow in those hard months the seed was sewn. We just literally did whatever we wanted and absolutely nothing happened. Maybe there and then I knew deep down the path of a straight and narrow life was just not going to work. Without realizing it at the time my subconscious mind had already taken a decision.

1985 came to an end and into 1986 and the last six months of service in the "Ops Room", the violence continued to escalate, we continued to look the other way. The guys down the beach went from strength to strength, I went from strength to strength. I surfed more and more, it all started falling into place.

I had a crystal clear focus and the desire to add to the small amount of natural talent I had at surfing. Surfing made me happy, it was an absolutely individual activity, something you could never dominate. I decided I would dedicate a lot more time to competition.

In June 1986, my two years term of National Service was over.

I went from a boy to a man in twenty four months, my innocence gone.

We had all most probably crossed a line and we would never ever be able to return.

XX
"INTO THE BLUE AGAIN, IN THE SILENT WATER"

We ran, Bullo and I, we ran like our very lives depended on it, and maybe it did. Fifty eight seconds from the first bang to the second, Maurice had been clear. I remembered now get out of there if the time gap was more than sixty seconds. So, we ran, it was exactly five years, five months and eight days since I had felt danger, real danger. The, I might get killed here, kind of danger.

The bull had lost the pack and had turned back, we were trapped between bulls still chasing us and now a bull coming straight back towards us. As if by some kind of magic trick suddenly we were alone, people had just vanished into doorways, cracks in the wall, climbed up drain pipes, they were gone, it was Bullo, myself and the bulls.

We ran. A slipping, sliding, adrenaline charged, un co-ordinated waving arms kind of run.

He got Bullo, just below the knee, his horn entered clean. In and out of his jeans, luckily just scraping a big red welt, but not penetrating the muscle. Bullo was a few paces behind me, law of the jungle 101, never go into the bush if you are the slowest. He had Bullo locked and loaded and he tossed him right over my head. Bullo flew through the air and thudded into the cobbles stones right in front of me, I was now next in line. We were almost at the end of the run, the bull ring was in sight when I dived for cover.

The route of the bull run is carefully barriered, to keep the bulls on course and the general public safe. There are two rows of thick sturdy horizontal wooden barriers, not solid walls a fence with parallel wooden planks with enough space to clearly see through, but not enough space for a bull to be able to jump or charge through. There is probably about a half a metre gap between the first plank and the floor, I slid under the plank into the safe zone like a runner into home base to win the world series. A head first, arms outstretched, full speed dive.

The bull hit the plank seconds behind me, at full charge. The impact and sound was tremendous, Bullo had made it behind the barrier as well, the bull only had eyes for me now. The bull snorted and scraped at me he was hell bent on getting to me, a bloody spray flew from his nostrils and a red drool poured out of his mouth. By this time first aid and security had reached us behind the first line of protection. I looked at Bullo, we did not have to say a word, we looked at the ring across the intersection and we both leaped over the top of the barrier and back into the road and we ran.

There is a slight downward incline just before you enter the big red doors of the "Plaza de Toros", a statue of Hemingway guards the entrance. We were the very last people still out on the road, just us and the one death bull as we made our last dash, to finish what we had started, what seemed hours ago.

As we ran down the slope towards those huge big red doors, the bull snorting and gaining ground on us with every step, I swear the doors slowly at first then ever faster started to close, what the hell were they doing, surely they would not leave us stranded?

At the very last moment we rushed through the gap and burst into the sandy brightness of the stadium, it was packed to the brim, everyone had crowded into the round arena, the elevated stadium seats filled to overflowing. The bull burst in seconds after us but was immediately met by a set of fully clothed bullfighters who herded him across the ring into the holding pens for that night`s bullfights. His last day had only just begun.

It had taken exactly five years, five months and eight days for me to feel the fear of real danger again.

Standing in the Plaza de Toros in Pamplona, twenty thousand people cheering and shouting, it hit me like a storm.

I liked it.

I suppose it all started way back in hospital, when I was just stuck in bed for such a long time. I eventually got a window bed which we raised so I could see out of the window. Addington hospital is right in front of the beach, prime time real estate, just across the road from Durban's South Beach and the place I learnt to surf. I just lay there all day and watched the ocean and visualised myself getting back out there and surfing again. I was also set up with a video recorder and given a few new VCR video tapes every day to watch. I am sure no one realised the pain I had to endure every time I laughed, but I ended up watching all the good funny movies of the time. Just another session of pleasure and pain, my reoccurring theme that was going to haunt me for the next thirty years.

National Lampoons Animal House was one of the movies I ended up watching. It became one of our cult movies and we watched it a thousand times. So, when my 21st birthday came along it was just a natural progression to make it a theme and Toga, Toga, Toga, party was the theme.

If you were not wearing a Toga you were not allowed in the front door. Rob was charged with making sure that was the way it was. He took it a step beyond, as he tends to do and made up his own rules. If you were wearing any kind of underwear under your toga, you were also not allowed in.

While the country was basically going up in flames, we just carried on like nothing was even going on, surfing, partying, just getting on with things.

The actual day of my birthday was during the week, Rob and I slept down at the beach on the pipe at Garvies and went for a dawn surf, it was, warm, glassy and fun, summer was on the way. At about six am I saw my whole family standing on the pipe, waving me in. They had prepared a champagne breakfast for me, which was a huge surprise. We scoffed down the food, skulled the champagne and went back surfing.

I guess that early morning champagne was what kicked it all off. It was a Thursday and we just did not stop drinking until the next Sunday morning.

I think it was those next few days that made me realise if you do stuff so absolutely outrageous, it`s kind of like it does not compute in most people´s brains and you can just end up getting away with it.

That weekend was outrageous. It was a big weekend and I broke every single rule I could. It all just blurred into chaos.

However, I do remember.

Rob checking to see if my mother was wearing underwear.
Rob and Gavin headbutting everyone before they could get in.
Rob starting things off with a bang by throwing all the food that had been prepared across the room.
The ensuing, food fight.
The party basically degenerating into a drunken orgy.
My parents coming home to find the house destroyed
Coming out of my bedroom to have Rob throw my chocolate birthday cake at me and miss.
Seeing said chocolate cake hit the wall and spray all down the passageway.
Going into the bathroom to find my brother standing on the edge of the bath urinating on an unknown naked female who had passed out in the bath.

Realising the whole downstairs of the house was under water.

Realising things had got completely out of hand and just carrying on.

Seeing Gavin pull the lounge curtains down so he could use them as a blanket as he passed out on the floor.

Being amazed at the fact there was no fight.

Anyone who was at that party would never, ever, ever forget it.

XXI
"AND YOU MAY ASK YOURSELF, WHAT IS THAT BEAUTIFUL HOUSE"

George came to pick me up at the airport just two days after coming out of surgery, the costs of staying were just too expensive. My travel insurance would not be paying, not one cent of the costs of the last few weeks in hospital. Financially I was ruined, I had no option but to face the facts and deal with my own healing process in my house up on the hill. It would be long and painful, this I knew with an absolute certainty, I had walked down this road before.

The worst was over, and yet the worst was just beginning.

I had not said anything to anyone and it terrified me, I could not remember.

My mind had gone blank, I had big voids of darkness in my head.

Not everything was gone, no, it was a selective loss of data. I could remember nearly everything, but then suddenly, I could not. A bit would be missing, a piece would be blank. If you have ever got up and gone to the fridge and opened the door and forgot what you wanted to get, well just like that, but with nearly everything. There were big chunks of darkness in my mind that would come and go. I knew I had a house in Spain, I could picture it clear as day, I just had no idea where it was!!!!!!!

Had the cables in my brain shorted out, like the priest who was next to me in my ward, was it the bang on my head, was it the lack of oxygen from such a long time under the water, or was it just short term, an effect left over from the anaesthetic? My mind was in overdrive as we headed south down the N2 highway back to Jeffreys Bay. Deep, deep, down I knew I had to sort out my life, it was not going well lately. I needed to work out a lot of stuff, I was just not quite sure exactly what. I was still so tired, everything had mixed up into a world of fact and fiction.

In the back of my head David Byrne was still singing "And you may ask yourself where, does that highway lead to?" When the long straight two lane N2 highway before the Van Stadens pass merged and melted and became the long straight highway of the A1 heading into Porto.

Kilometres of tarmac forever imprinted into my brain, it would take a bit more than a bump on the head for me to ever forget how big an impact such an insignificant thing like a stretch of highway could have on the course of my life.

The off ramp was ahead, a slight right turn onto the IP-5, cross through central Spain and onwards to France for the last contest, and the end of year awards, say my goodbyes and then back home to Durban. Everything was in place, my future job, my future wife, it was all waiting, life was set.

It just happened, I was set on turning, I had taken my decision, of course I was turning but I just froze. My mind said turn right, my arms held course. I just drove right past everything I knew and headed straight north up the A1 and directly back to Ferrol. She was there.

I was driving towards the unknown, driving towards her and a new future.

Wayno was the first person I saw, I had not seen him in years, not since we were in the army, we had been inseparable, he had my back and I had his. Not turning that day on the A1 had led me to that moment, the hardest thing I had ever had to do, the consequence of not taking that exit and onto France, my job, my wedding.

I knew there would be consequences and I would have to face them, of course I knew, that had been whipped into us at school. Pleasure and pain, they always seemed to go hand in hand. Wayno was just sitting there that day, the one person I needed to see and there he was, miraculously it was him. I had just called off my wedding, it was only days away, the invitations had been sent, presents had arrived, the cake had been baked. Uncertainty had been eating me away, I so easily could have taken the established path and it would have been good, I am sure of that, it would have been fantastic. Wayno looked at me straight in the eye, he knew I was getting married, he did not flinch when I told him I had not less than five minutes earlier walked away from everything. He looked me straight in the eye and said, "brother do what your soul tells you", and that is exactly what I did.

She was on the other side of the world, so I went to her. She was waiting.

George snapped me back, the pain was incredible, "Are you sure you will be alright, alone?" he asked as we took the offramp into Jeffreys Bay. I had forgotten the house had been burgled and most of the furniture had been stolen, luckily the beds were still there, they must have been too big to take. "I will be fine" I replied, but I was terrified, terrified that I could not remember, terrified she had not come. I knew what that meant, I could not face that reality just yet. One battle at a time, I still had a very long road to recovery ahead.

I would sort things out. Lately life had slipped out of control. My wife was threatening to throw me out. I had almost stopped doing the one thing that really made me happy, surfing. All I did was work all day, I never seemed to have time for my boys. I needed to make it. I had my family depending on me. I had a lot to sort out. I had a beautiful daughter in France, I really needed to see her soon.

Meanwhile the Talking Heads turned up the volume in my brain.

THE END IS THE BEGINNING

Footnotes.

1

"A referendum was held in South Africa on 17 March 1992. The referendum was limited to white South African voters, who were asked whether or not they supported the negotiated reforms begun by F.W. De Klerk the then State President. The referendum proposed to end the Apartheid System that had been implemented since 1948."

"The result of the election was a large victory for the "yes" side, which ultimately resulted in apartheid being abolished"

69% of the white population voted in favour.

2

"What is a Tokolosh"

in Zulu mythology the Tokolosh is a dwarf like water sprite. It is considered a mischievous and evil spirit that can become invisible by drinking water. Tokoloshs are called upon by malevolent people to cause trouble for others. At its least harmful a tokolosh can be used to scare children, but its power extends to causing illness or even the death of the victim. The creature might be banished by a nánga (spiritual healer), who has the power to expel it from the area.

Another explanation is that the Tokolosh resembles a zombie, poltergeist, or gremlin, created by South African shamans who have been offended by someone. The Tokolosh may also wander, causing mischief wherever it goes, particularly to schoolchildren. Other details include its gremlin-like appearance and gouged out eyes

"Some Zulu people (and other southern African tribes) are still superstitious when it comes to things like the supposedly fictional Tokolosh—a hairy creature created by a wizard to harm his enemies (also ... known to rape women and bite off sleeping people's toes)

According to legend, the only way to keep the Tokolosh away at night is to put a brick beneath each leg of one's bed. However, this will not protect anything but the person whose bed it is along with the bed itself, as it may instead cause havoc not involving said people. They get their power from a hot poker thrust into the crown of the body during creation.

"INTO THE BLUE AGAIN"

"It´s not something you can control, it's a feeling that creeps into your stomach, deep down inside of you. When you see her, the hair on your arms stands on end, you feel a whole number of emotions all at once.

No matter how many times you see her, no matter how many times, it´s always that same feeling, an uncontrollable urge to be with her always, but life is cruel sometimes and no matter how many nights you dream of waking up and seeing her in all her glory, destiny keeps you apart.

No matter how many days pass without her I know it is just a question of time, before I see her again, even if for just few brief moments, she is mine again.

Hope is what keeps me moving forward every day.

That same destiny that brought you together now keeps us apart, but she can never leave. She is always there. No one can ever take her away from me, she is a part of me.

From that very first moment I laid eyes on her, I have felt her close to me.

Like most eternal love affairs, it is more a lusty need at first, a primal urge to see her again, as soon as possible, a need to be near her, to feel her energy to be absorbed by her.

With time that need has eased and has evolved into just a warm feeling of trust, I know she is there, she is not going anywhere, she is patiently waiting for me.

I love her smell, I love her beauty, I love her touch, there is only one like her, I have looked the world over and I cannot find anything that even comes close to her, she truly is unique and I need her.

We have had our ups and our downs, of course we have, like all jealous lovers she has even tried to kill me.

We have had some great times, the best of times. Important times, key moments, moments that mark a lifetime.

Ever since that very first day, I have moved heaven and earth to be with her, she has been good to me, she has been amazing, even the trying to kill me.

I have made it my mission to make sure she is part of me, and I have succeeded.

From that very first day we have been together far too little, but we have been together as often as possible, just one day with her is better than a thousand with another.

I am eternally grateful to have surfing in my life."

Clyde Martin.

Printed in Great Britain
by Amazon